BOOK TWO
THE
WINNING
EDGE
SERIES

Out in the Cold

Published in Nashville, Tennessee, by Tommy Nelson™, a division of Thomas Nelson, Inc.

Unless otherwise indicated, Scripture quotations are from the *International Children's Bible, New Century Version,* copyright © 1983, 1986, 1988.

Author's acknowledgments: Sarah Kirby, Scott Kirby, Megan McAndrew, Kay McAndrew, and Tami Mickle.

Executive Editor: Laura Minchew; Managing Editor: Beverly Phillips. Book Design by Kandi Shepherd.

Library of Congress Cataloging-in-Publication Data
Kirby, Lynn. 1956–
    Out in the Cold / by Lynn Kirby.
        p. cm.—(The winning edge series ; 2)
    Summary: While trying to keep up with her friends in the field of competitive ice skating, Shannon struggles to trust God with her problems.
    1ISBN 0-8499-5836-9
    [1. Ice skating—Fiction. 2. Christian life—Fiction.]
I. Title. II. Series: Kirby, Lynn, 1956–   Winning edge series : 2.
PZ7.K6335230u 1998
[Fic]—dc21

                                    98–5571
                                      CIP
                                      AC

Printed in the United States of America
98 99 00 01 02 DHC 9 8 7 6 5 4 3 2 1

BOOK TWO
THE
WINNING
EDGE
SERIES

Out in the Cold

Lynn Kirby

Tommy
NELSON

Thomas Nelson, Inc.
Nashville

For Betty, in fulfillment of
a promise made long ago.

Figure Skating Terms

Boards—The barrier around the ice surface is often referred to as "the boards."

Choreography—The arrangement of dance to music. In figure skating, it would be figure skating moves to music.

Crossovers—While going forward or backward, the skater crosses one foot over the other.

Edges—The skate blade has two sharp edges with a slight hollow in the middle. The edge on the outside of the foot is called the "outside edge." The edge on the inside of the foot is called the "inside edge."

Footwork—A series of turns, steps, and positions executed while moving across the ice.

Jumps

Axel—A jump that takes off from a forward outside edge. The skater makes one and a half turns in the air to land on a back outside edge of the opposite foot. A *Double Axel Jump* is the same as the axel, but the skater rotates two and a half times in the air. For a *Triple Axel,* the skater rotates three and one half times.

Ballet Jump—From a backward outside edge, the skater taps the ice behind with the toe pick, and springs into the air, turning forward. The jump appears as a simple, graceful leap, landing forward.

Bunny Hop—A beginner jump. The skater springs forward from one foot, touches down with the toe pick of the other foot, and lands on the original foot going forward.

Combination Jump—The skater performs two or more jumps without making a turn or step in between.

Flip Jump—From a back inside edge, the skater takes off by thrusting a toe pick into the ice behind her, vaults into the air where she makes a full turn, and lands on the back outside edge of the other foot. A *Double Flip Jump* is the same as the flip jump, but with two rotations. For a *Triple Flip,* the skater makes three rotations.

Loop Jump—The skater takes off from a back outside edge, makes a full turn in the air, and lands on the same back outside edge. A *Double Loop Jump* is the same as the loop jump, but the skater rotates two times. For a *Triple Loop Jump,* the skater completes three rotations.

Lutz Jump—Similar to the flip jump except the skater takes off from a back outside edge, thrusts a toe pick into the ice, makes a full turn in the air, and lands on the back outside edge of the other foot. Usually done in the corner. A *Double Lutz Jump* is the same as the lutz jump, but with two rotations. A *Triple Lutz Jump* is the same as the lutz jump, but the skater makes three full rotations.

Salchow Jump—The skater takes off from a back inside edge, makes a full turn in the air, and lands on the back outside edge of the other foot. A *Double Salchow* is the same as the salchow, but the skater makes two full rotations. For a *Triple Salchow,* the skater makes three rotations.

Toe Loop Jump—The skater takes off from a back outside edge assisted by a toe pick thrust, makes a full turn in the air, and lands on the back outside edge of the same foot. A *Double Toe Loop* is the same as the toe loop jump, but with two rotations. For a *Triple Toe Loop,* the skater makes three full rotations.

Waltz Jump—The skater takes off from a forward outside edge, makes a half turn, and lands on the back outside edge of the other foot.

Moves in the Field—Figure skaters must pass a series of tests in order to advance to each competitive level. These tests consist of stroking, edges, and turns skated in prescribed patterns. Sometimes referred to as Field Moves.

Spins

Camel Spin—A spin in an arabesque position.

Combination Spin—The skater changes from one position to another while continuing to spin.

Flying Camel—A flying spin. The skater jumps from a forward outside edge and lands in a camel position rotating on the backward outside edge of the opposite foot.

Layback Spin—A spin that is completed with the skater's head and shoulders leaning backward with the free leg bent behind in an "attitude" position.

One-foot Spin—An upright spin on one foot.

Sit Spin—A spin performed in a "sitting" position, on a bent knee with the free leg extended in front.

Two-foot Spin—The first spin a skater learns. The skater uses both feet.

Shoot-the-duck—One leg is extended in front while the skater glides on a deeply bent knee.

Skate Guards—Rubber protectors worn over skating blades when walking off ice. Also called blade guards.

Spiral—The skater glides down the ice on one foot with the free leg extended high in back.

Spread Eagle—The skater glides on two feet with toes pointed outward.

Stroking—Pushing with one foot, then the other, to glide across the ice.

Three-turn—A turn on one foot from forward to backward or backward to forward. Traces a "3" on the ice.

Toe Picks—The sharp teeth on the front of the figure skating blade. Used to assist in turns, jumps, and spins.

Zamboni—The large machine used to make the ice surface smooth.

One

"Okay, Shannon, let's try that flip jump* again."

It was Wednesday afternoon, and twelve-year-old Shannon Roberts was in the middle of a skating lesson with her coach, Susan Barnes. Shannon was small for her age. Her medium-length black hair and dark eyes showed her Korean heritage.

Shannon made a three-turn* on her left foot to set up the jump. Skating backward on a left inside edge*, she extended her right leg behind her while deeply bending her left knee. Jabbing her right toe pick* into the ice, she vaulted into the air and made a full turn before landing smoothly on her right blade. Shannon extended her arms and held her position for a few seconds to "check out" of the jump. "Perfect!" she said.

Her coach nodded, but said nothing. Shannon knew better than to hope for a word of praise; figure skating

*An asterisk in the text indicates a figure skating term that is in the list of definitions on pages v-viii.

1

coaches are not known for flattering their students. Coach Barnes was young and pretty, with brown eyes and long brown hair, which she usually pulled back into a ponytail. She was also a demanding coach who expected a lot from her students.

"Well, that's all for today," Coach Barnes said, looking at her watch. She adjusted her coat as she headed off the ice. "It's coming along, Shannon. Keep working on it; and work on your one-foot spin*! Next week I'll get you started on the lutz jump*."

The lutz? Shannon couldn't help feeling pleased. After she mastered the lutz, she could begin working on an axel*, which was the hardest jump of all.

Shannon knew that twelve years old was a little late to begin a serious skating career. Many kids start when they are only four or five. However, until the new ice rink opened just a few months before, skating had been just an impossible dream.

Now that she finally had the opportunity to skate, Shannon was making up for lost time. In just a few months, she had mastered the basic levels and was working on jumps and spins. She had even participated in her first competition, winning a second place medal.

Shannon watched to be sure her coach disappeared into the coaches' room before she got off the ice to take a quick break. She slipped on her skate guards* and then fished her water bottle out of her skate bag and took a long drink. On the ice, her friend Kristen Grant was setting up for a double axel*. From a forward edge, Kristen launched into the air, turning counterclockwise two and a half times before crashing into the ice.

Oh, that was so close! Shannon thought. Kristen, a tall girl with curly auburn hair, was the same age as Shannon, but she was already an experienced competitive skater. Kristen had taken skating lessons for years. For several months she had been working on a double axel, but she had not yet landed one.

"Better give up, Kris!" Kristen's twin brother, Kevin, offered his usual encouragement as he skated near her. Kevin was a good skater, in spite of the fact that he didn't believe in working hard. Shannon wondered how good he would be if he ever really practiced. Shannon thought Kevin was one of the best-looking guys in school. She liked his bright red hair and freckles, although he complained about being called "carrot top."

"Kevin!" yelled Tiffany, Shannon's six-year-old sister, as she tugged at Kevin's sweatshirt. Tiffany was a rink favorite; but sometimes she and her friends could be pests to Shannon and her friends.

Kevin turned to her good-naturedly. "Hey, Squirt! What's up?"

Tiffany giggled. "Watch me!" She demonstrated a two-foot spin*.

When she finished, Kevin clapped and cheered, "Cool, Tiff!"

Shannon liked the way Kevin treated her little sister. She was sure most boys wouldn't have been so nice.

"Have you already finished?" A slender girl with a long pale blond ponytail and hazel eyes stepped off the ice and sat down next to Shannon. Amy Pederson was also Shannon's age, and like Kristen, she was an experienced competitive skater. After Mr. Pederson had a terrible accident, Amy's family had come to Walton so her grandparents could help take care of her father while he was recovering from his injuries. Until her father was able to work again, Amy had struggled to earn money for skating by baby-sitting. Shannon would never forget the special way God had answered Amy's prayers.

"Are you sure Coach Grischenko won't get mad?" teased Shannon. Amy's coach, Elena Grischenko, was a famous Ukrainian skating instructor with strict standards and a hot temper. She did not approve of resting.

Amy scanned the rink sheepishly. "I think I saw her go into the coaches' room." She took a deep breath. "Anyway, I need a break. I don't think I can take one more fall on that double lutz*." The double lutz was one of the most difficult double jumps.

"My coach said I could start on my lutz jump next week," said Shannon.

Amy smiled. "Way to go!"

Shannon looked at her wistfully. "*I* wish I was working on a *double* lutz."

"At the rate you're going, it won't be long!" Amy assured her. "You're learning so much faster than I did at first. Before you know it, you'll be beating everybody in competitions."

4

"That'll be the day!" Shannon was a little embarrassed. She knew it would be a long time before her skating was up to the level of her friend, but it made her feel good to know Amy had confidence in her ability.

"Is this a party?" Kristen stopped in front of the boards* with a spray of ice.

"Just a break!" said Amy.

"Watch out! Coach Grischenko will *break* you, if you're not careful," warned Kristen with a smile. As usual, she looked elegant in a simple green skating dress that set off her creamy complexion and brown eyes. "And I don't want her angry for my lesson."

Amy laughed. "It's getting too crowded to do much during this session."

"That's true," agreed Kristen, looking at the skaters whizzing past on the ice. "Remember when the rink first opened? Hardly anybody came here. Even Kevin is complaining about how crowded it's been lately."

"It looks like a lot of people have discovered skating," said Shannon.

"Who's that girl over there?" asked Amy, pointing to an African-American girl wearing a skating dress. The girl was very pretty, of medium height, and slender. Her black hair was plaited in dozens of tiny braids and pulled back away from her face.

Kristen turned to look. "I don't know. I've never seen her before."

"That's a cool skating dress," said Amy, admiring the unusual tie-dyed dress the girl was wearing. "I wonder who she is."

Kristen shrugged. "My coach said something about some more skaters coming here for lessons."

"That's cool," said Amy. "We need a few more skaters around here—you know, some who can really skate. Not just ones who crowd the ice and fall down!"

Now, what did that *mean?* thought Shannon. She wasn't sure she liked the tone in Amy's voice. *I wonder if they think I'm not good enough to hang around with them?* But she didn't say anything.

"Why aren't you skating?" asked a little voice. It was Tiffany.

"We're just taking a break," explained Shannon.

"I don't ever take breaks," said Tiffany, her nose in the air. "I practice hard all the time."

"No, you don't," countered Shannon.

"Do, too," said Tiffany as she put her hands on her hips, preparing for an argument.

But Kristen interrupted. "We *all* better get back to work." Then she turned and stepped back on the ice.

Amy slipped off her skate guards and followed, but Shannon continued to watch the new girl on the ice for a few minutes. The girl handled herself with the kind of confidence that comes from years of skating. As soon as she stepped on the ice, she began stroking* around the rink, building up speed. She turned easily backward and began doing crossovers*, covering the length of the rink in a few swift strokes.

Wow! thought Shannon. It was obvious that the girl was a very good skater.

Once Shannon was back on the ice, she found it hard to concentrate on her skating. She couldn't help thinking about what Amy had said—about the rink needing more good skaters. She knew she wasn't as good a skater as her friends. Maybe they didn't like hanging around with her.

Amy and Kristen had helped her learn to skate. They had encouraged her to enter her first competition, and they helped her get her program ready. Amy had even given her an old pair of used skates and loaned her a costume for the competition.

Still, as nice as they had been, Shannon knew that the two girls spent more time together than they did with her. She had never thought much about it before, but now she realized that they liked to practice together at the rink, getting advice from each other about their jumps and spins—things Shannon hadn't even been taught yet.

After stroking around the rink several times, she decided to work on her one-foot spin. Shannon skated backward crossovers, right foot over left, making a circle on the ice. Stepping into the imaginary circle with her left foot, she rotated slowly at first, bringing her arms and right foot slowly in to increase her speed.

Just as she began to feel in control of the spin, she was startled by a skater landing a huge jump directly in front of her. Afraid of being hit, Shannon abandoned the spin quickly. But she was so surprised that she fell and twisted her ankle. She looked up to see who could be so rude. It was that new girl, which made Shannon angry. *I always stop to see if the other skater is okay in an accident,* she thought.

Annoyed, she limped over to the side to inspect the damage. Her ankle seemed to be okay, but it would probably be sore for a day or two. She looked up to see the new girl continuing to skate at high speed around the ice. "She could have stopped to say she was sorry," Shannon mumbled to herself.

"Resting?" asked Coach Barnes, frowning at her.

"I think I twisted my ankle," she explained.

"Can you walk on it?" asked the coach.

"Yeah."

"Hmm . . . put some ice on it," she said and skated off toward another one of her students. Shannon checked out her ankle. It was a little sore, but it seemed okay.

It was almost time to go anyway, so Shannon slipped on her skate guards and headed into the lobby to take off her skates. Tiffany had already gotten off the ice and was clowning around with some of her friends in the lobby. When they saw Shannon, they whispered something among themselves and rolled their eyes.

Shannon glanced back to see if Amy and Kristen were ready to go, but to her surprise, they were standing by the boards talking to that new girl.

Shannon considered joining them, but she was tired and her ankle hurt. Right now she didn't want to meet anybody—especially that girl.

Shannon unlaced her skates and reached into her

bag for her water bottle. She took a deep drink and then started coughing. "Yuck," she yelled. "This isn't water! It's . . . it's . . . pickle juice!" Then she heard Tiffany and her friends giggling. She turned to see them standing in the corner.

"Her face! Her face! Did you see her face?" the three girls chanted as they doubled over in laughter.

"Tiffany," scolded Shannon. "Where did you get—"

"That's for me to know and you to find out," teased Tiffany as she headed back toward the ice.

"Tiffany, come back here! We've got to go," she yelled.

"In a minute," Tiffany yelled back.

Shannon took off her skates and hobbled over to the water fountain. "Little sisters," she mumbled, and rinsed out her mouth.

She turned to see Amy and Kristen jump off the ice. "Shannon, you've got to meet Jamie!" said Amy excitedly, as she sat down and pulled a pair of sneakers out of her skate bag. She looked around. "That's funny. I thought she was right behind us."

The air was suddenly punctuated with a yell from the direction of the video games, and the girls turned to see Jamie there with Kevin.

Kristen shook her head. "Oh, no. Kevin is corrupting her already."

"What did you find out about her?" Shannon asked.

"Her name is Jamie Summers," said Kristen. "She just moved here from Atlanta."

"I haven't seen her in school," said Shannon.

"She goes to private school. You should go look at Coach Grischenko's schedule. She's on it every day and sometimes twice a day," said Kristen.

"Wow," Shannon said. "I wish my parents cared about my skating that much."

"Yeah. Her teachers work around her skating competitions, as long as she gets high grades and stuff," Amy said, then added, "and she's a really good skater." She turned to Kristen. "Are you going to go to that competition in Dallas?"

"Yeah," said Kristen, "if Coach Grischenko says it's okay."

"Me, too. It's going to be so cool!" said Amy. "I hope Coach Grischenko will let us both do it."

"My coach hasn't said anything about it to me yet," said Shannon. "Maybe she'll let me compete, too."

"I don't know, Shannon," said Amy. "This is a much bigger and harder competition than last time."

"Oh." Shannon wasn't sure what to say. *Didn't her friends want her to compete?* "When is the competition?"

"In just a few weeks or so. We're going to have to really work hard to be ready in time," Kristen said.

Shannon didn't want to hear any more about the competition. Or about Jamie. She just wanted to get away. She looked around for her little sister. Tiffany stood there with one skate off and one skate on, talking to a friend.

"Tiff, stop talking and let's go," scolded Shannon.

"Wait a minute," whined Tiffany as she pulled off

her other skate and stuffed it into her bag. "Why are you in such a hurry?"

"Mom's waiting. Bye, guys," Shannon called to her friends. "See ya at school tomorrow. Come on, Tiff," she yelled as she hurried out of the rink.

Tiffany grabbed her bag and followed her, shouting as she went. "Wait up, Shannon!"

❅ ❅ ❅ ❅ ❅

On the way home, Shannon thought about the competition in Dallas. Amy and Kristen would be going. Jamie would probably go, too. She wasn't sure she really wanted to take part, but she hated being left out.

Shannon couldn't believe Amy and Kristen had deserted her for this new girl. Was it because Jamie was such a good skater? Maybe they only thought of Shannon as a beginner.

I wish I had started skating years ago, Shannon thought wistfully. *Then I could be going to big competitions like Amy and Kristen!*

Two

Shannon had been taking ballet classes since she was eight years old, and she loved it. When the ice rink opened in Walton, she hadn't really expected her parents to allow her to do both. But when they agreed, Tiffany had begged for skating lessons, too. Now they were both taking skating lessons.

Shannon had been thrilled when she met Amy and Kristen, both advanced figure skaters. They had promised to help her learn to skate, and they'd lived up to their promise. With their help and weekly private lessons with her coach, Shannon had progressed very quickly.

Still, Shannon realized that she would never catch up to the level of her friends. But she couldn't stop thinking about Kristen and Amy's competition. Although she knew she wasn't really ready for a competition this soon, especially a big competition like the one in Dallas, she hated being the only one who couldn't go. As she prepared for her ballet class on Thursday afternoon, she considered the problem.

"Hurry up, Shannon!" Mrs. Roberts tapped on Shannon's door. "It's almost time to leave."

"I'll be ready in a few minutes, Mom!" she yelled. Shannon skated on Monday, Wednesday, and Friday afternoons; she had ballet class on Tuesdays and Thursdays. She pulled her dark hair into a small knot and secured it with several bobby pins. Usually, she dressed at Madame Junot's studio, but today Shannon's mother had to run some errands so she'd told Shannon to dress at home. She covered her black leotard and light pink tights with a long sweatshirt.

Shannon checked her ballet bag to be sure she had her soft leather ballet slippers and toe shoes. Madame Junot did not have any patience with forgetfulness. Shannon groaned, remembering the last time she displeased her dance teacher. Madame had scolded her in front of the whole class for failing to hold a proper position during an exercise. Even worse, she had insisted the entire class practice the same exercise over and over. It was so embarrassing.

Shannon's ankle ached and she reached down to massage it. She wondered whether she would be able to dance. Cautiously, she tested it, trying to determine if it was strong enough. Fortunately, the ankle seemed only sore. She decided not to mention it to her mother, hoping she could make it through dance class without any problems.

As Shannon rubbed her ankle, her resentment toward Jamie grew. Surely a skater as good as Jamie knew better than to land a jump near someone doing a spin! *Some people think they own the ice!* she thought.

✳ ✳ ✳ ✳ ✳

Shannon's mother was tall with dark hair and serious blue eyes. She was patient and kind, but she also had an air of authority. "You're awfully quiet today, Shannon. Is everything all right?"

Shannon didn't answer right away. She wasn't sure her parents would understand about the competition. Her mother did not always see things the way she did. She sometimes wondered if it was because she had been adopted. Shannon had come from Korea to live with her adoptive parents when she was only eight months old. Six years later, her parents had also adopted her little sister from Korea.

However, Shannon knew she needed to have her parents' support in any decision she made about skating. She took a deep breath and plunged in. "Mom, there's a big skating competition coming up in Dallas. Everyone else is going. Do you think I could go?"

Her mother frowned. "You just competed a few weeks ago."

"I know, but Amy and Kristen are going."

"Does your coach think you should compete?"

Shannon hesitated. Coach Barnes hadn't even mentioned the competition to her, but Shannon felt sure her coach would say it was okay. "Um, I only just found out about it yesterday, but I'm sure she'll want me to do it."

Mrs. Roberts sighed and shook her head. "I don't know, Shannon. It seems to me you have enough to do right now. Did you forget the spring ballet recital?"

The spring recital! Shannon had almost forgotten. There were probably going to be extra rehearsals, and they would interfere with skating practice.

"No, but I can use my *Star Wars* program for the figure skating competition. There wouldn't be much to learn." Shannon looked pleadingly at her mother.

"Shannon, you can't do everything. Right now I think you've got your hands full. There will be other competitions."

"I could quit ballet," Shannon quietly offered. As soon as she said it she wondered if she really meant that. She loved dance, but right now the skating competition seemed like the most important thing in the world.

Her mother sighed. "Shannon, it's fine to skate for fun, but you've already spent many years in ballet training. It would be a waste to throw that away."

Having suggested dropping ballet, Shannon felt she couldn't back down. "It wouldn't be a waste. Lots of skaters take ballet. It helps their skating to be more artistic."

"Madame Junot thinks you show promise."

"How do you know I couldn't be good at skating, too?" Shannon complained. "Amy and Kristen said that I've learned as much in the last six months as they did in two years!"

"Look, Shannon," said her mother sternly, "you can keep skating for now, but I don't want to hear any more about quitting ballet."

Shannon didn't say anything. It was just like her mother to see everything from a strictly practical side. On the other hand, she was secretly relieved that her mother hadn't taken her seriously about quitting ballet. She knew she didn't really want to quit, but she was determined to enter that competition.

Somehow she would find a way.

✳ ✳ ✳ ✳ ✳

By the time Shannon's ballet class was over her ankle really hurt. In the dressing room, she took off her ballet slipper and massaged her foot.

"Are you okay?" asked Darcy O'Neal, a tall, thin girl who had recently transferred to Madame Junot's academy from another ballet school.

"I hurt my ankle ice-skating yesterday," said Shannon, while she put on her regular shoes.

"How long have you skated?"

"I just started a few months ago."

"Cool," said Darcy, looking impressed.

Shannon hadn't had much of a chance to really get to know Darcy, but she liked her.

"Skating's fun," said Shannon. "Maybe you could come sometime."

Darcy grinned. "Yeah, sprained ankles sound like lots of fun!"

"Oh, this was an accident," said Shannon.

"Like someone would sprain her ankle on purpose," said Darcy, then she laughed.

Shannon laughed, too. "I'll teach you to skate without accidents," she offered.

Darcy looked doubtful. "I'll think about it."

Shannon hoped Darcy would decide to come sometime. *It would be fun,* she thought.

❄ ❄ ❄ ❄ ❄

By the time Shannon got home her ankle was beginning to swell. *Maybe they won't notice,* thought Shannon. But she had barely walked in the door when her mother said to her father, "Jim, take a look at Shannon's ankle."

Jim Roberts was a physician with an office in Walton. Tall and angular, with sandy blond hair and green eyes, he looked totally different from his daughters. After examining her ankle, he pronounced, "No skating tomorrow."

❄ ❄ ❄ ❄ ❄

Shannon sat down for supper, and her father gently propped her foot on a chair. Using a bag of frozen peas as an ice pack, he gingerly wrapped her ankle.

Shannon groaned. It was tough to have to miss a practice just now. *This is all Jamie's fault,* she thought to herself. *I wish she had stayed in Atlanta!*

"Shannon, I'm a little concerned," began her father. "Maybe the skating and ballet are too much for you."

"No! It's not too much!" Shannon shook her head

vigorously. "I can do it. Anyway, Amy and Kristen train for hours every day, and they do all right."

"I'm not worried about Amy and Kristen." Mr. Roberts's voice was firm. "We allowed you to begin skating lessons because we thought it might be fun for you to learn a new sport, but you're taking it too seriously. You've only been skating for a few months, and you've already been in one competition. Now your mother tells me you want to enter another."

"But I love skating!" protested Shannon. Without thinking, she pulled her ankle off the chair. "Ooh!" she said, flinching in pain.

Her parents exchanged glances.

Replacing the ice pack on her foot, Shannon looked up. "I can keep up with everything. I know I can!"

Her father thought for a moment. "Well, we'll see. Shannon, we've heard nothing but 'ballet' and 'dancing' for years. Now you tell us you want to quit?"

"You sound just like Mom!" Shannon pouted.

"We don't mind if you keep skating for a while," said her mother, "but let's take things a little slower."

Tiffany piped up, "Yeah, I'm supposed to be the skater in the family. You're supposed to be the ballerina."

Shannon gave her sister a mean look.

"That's enough, Tiffany," said Mr. Roberts. Turning to Shannon, he said, "It's your decision if you want to quit ballet, but you need to give it a lot more thought. We'll see how you feel in a few months." He winked at her. "And in the meantime, take care of that ankle."

Shannon knew the subject was closed for the present. *Oh, well, at least they're still letting me skate. I'll just have to prove I can do both. If I could enter that competition and win, maybe then they'd see that I can dance and skate!*

❅ ❅ ❅ ❅ ❅

Shannon went to school as usual on Friday, but with a note excusing her from the volleyball game in PE class. She didn't mind missing that, but it was tough staying home from skating practice after school. Stuck on the sofa with her ankle propped up, Shannon watched miserably as Tiffany headed out the door for the rink.

Tiffany lugged a large skate bag behind her. "Bye, Shannon!" she called out mischievously. "I'm glad *I* don't have to wear a package of peas!"

Shannon grabbed one of the sofa pillows and threw it at her sister, who disappeared through the door just in time.

She had some history homework due on Monday, and she might as well get it done. Shannon limped to her room and sat down at her desk. After staring at her homework for a few minutes, she put down the notebook. All she could think of was skating and ballet.

Shannon's cat rubbed up against her sore ankle. "Meow!"

"Ouch," she said. "Buttons, what is it?" she asked, annoyed. But when she picked him up he began to purr softly and she gently stroked his gray coat.

Shannon glanced around her room. Ballerina dolls and figurines lined her bookshelves, and there was a huge framed poster advertising *The Nutcracker* ballet. There was not a single doll, figure, or poster representing skating. Amy had a huge collection of skating figurines and souvenirs, including a large case of competition medals.

Shannon picked up her cat and held him close. "Someday I'm going to have as many as Amy," she told him. "Just wait and see."

❋ ❋ ❋ ❋ ❋

Shannon had managed to complete some of her homework when Tiffany popped in wearing a new skating dress.

"Do you like my new dress, Shannon?" asked Tiffany, while she twirled around. It was light blue with a white underskirt and white lace trim on the neck and sleeves. "Mommy bought it for me at the rink today."

"Mom bought you *another* skating dress? You've already got more dresses than I do!"

"But you have both ballet *and* skating clothes," said Tiffany smugly. "Anyway, Mommy said it was so pretty she just couldn't resist." She pranced over to the full-length mirror and inspected her reflection.

"Mom!" Shannon limped to the door and called loudly into the hallway.

Mrs. Roberts appeared in the hall holding a dish-towel.

"Mom, why did you get Tiffany a new skating dress?" Shannon complained. "That's not fair! She already has more practice dresses than I have!"

Mrs. Roberts sighed. "The dress is not new. I got it at the used equipment sale at the rink."

"Couldn't you have looked for one for me?"

Mrs. Roberts shook her head. "I did. There weren't any your size, except for one that looked very shabby."

Shannon frowned. "I still don't think it's fair. You care more about Tiffany's skating than you do mine."

Mrs. Roberts propped her hands on her hips. "We're through discussing this issue, Shannon."

Shannon opened her mouth to argue, but the look in her mother's eyes stopped her before she could utter a word. She knew better than to talk back.

Tiffany disappeared, and Shannon went back to her homework, but it was hard to concentrate. She stared unseeing at the assigned questions, her head full of a bigger problem: how to convince her parents she was truly serious about skating.

Three

Shannon thought the weekend would never end. She couldn't wait to get back on the ice on Monday afternoon. Before school on Monday morning, her father examined her ankle. Shannon held her breath as he carefully inspected it, his face serious.

Finally, he put her foot down. "The swelling is completely gone," he said. "You can skate this afternoon." Shannon's face erupted in a smile, but her father added sternly, "On two conditions: If your ankle begins to hurt, promise me you'll get off the ice."

"Yes, sir." Shannon nodded, pleased just to have permission to skate.

"And no jumping today. All right?"

"No jumping?" Shannon frowned. "But my ankle doesn't even hurt anymore."

"No jumping," her father repeated.

"All right," sighed Shannon. This sore ankle had already cost two days of skating practice. Now she couldn't work on jumps, and the competition was not far away. That is, if she could convince her parents and her coach to allow her to enter.

＊ ＊ ＊ ＊ ＊

School—especially science class—seemed to last forever that day. Mr. Terino lectured for nearly the entire hour on the human digestive system and assigned twenty vocabulary words for homework. Shannon thought the school day would never end.

When Shannon and her sister arrived at the rink that afternoon, Amy and Kristen were already there with their skates on. However, the girls were intent on watching someone on the ice. They hardly noticed when Shannon and Tiffany came in. Shannon put down her skate bag and walked toward the girls.

"What's going on?" asked Shannon. "Has the session already started?"

Amy turned around to greet them. "The public session hasn't started, but Jamie's on the ice."

Shannon joined her friends at the large plate glass window looking into the ice arena. Except for Coach Grischenko, Jamie was alone on the ice.

"She's so lucky! I'd love to have the ice all to myself sometime," said Amy.

Shannon wasn't sure if she would want to be on the ice alone. It sounded—well, *lonely*.

"I wish I had her schedule," said Kristen. "She can skate when the rink isn't busy."

"Her parents must be rich," said Shannon.

"I don't know. She lives with her mother," Amy said. "She's some kind of lawyer. I don't know what her dad does, but I don't think he lives here."

"Are they divorced?" asked Kristen.

"I don't know," said Amy.

"And she moved here just to train with the coach?" Shannon asked.

"No. But she said her mother did make sure there was a good coach in the area before she accepted the job," Kristen said.

Shannon turned around just in time to see Jamie land a spectacular jump. "That's a triple!" she said, amazed.

Kristen shook her head. "No, only a double. But it was really high and strong."

"I want to see!" said Tiffany excitedly. She climbed onto a bench to peer into the rink area. "Wow!" she exclaimed as she put her nose to the glass. "She's a *really* good skater!"

"I overheard Jamie's mother talking to Coach Grischenko," said Kristen. "She said something about Jamie winning a big championship last year."

"I remember seeing a picture in my skating magazine of a girl who won a regional championship," said Amy. "She looked a lot like Jamie."

"I wonder if that was her?" said Kristen.

As they watched, Jamie skated backward on a right outside edge, placed her left toe pick behind her, and thrust her toe pick into the ice. With that thrust, she vaulted into the air and spun for what seemed like ages before coming down on her right skate. The landing was rather sloppy, but the jump looked impressive.

"*That* was a triple, wasn't it?" asked Shannon.

"It was a triple toe loop*," said Kristen.

"I'm already jealous," said Amy. "I wish I was working on triple jumps."

"I can't even do a double jump," said Shannon.

"I can do double jumps!" said Tiffany as she jumped down from the bench.

"Tiffany, you can't do a double jump!" scolded Shannon.

"I can, too," she retorted. "See?" Tiffany jumped with all her might, making a three-quarter turn before landing on two feet on the floor. "See," she said. "I did it. I'm going to be like Jamie when I get big."

Kristen grinned. "Well, it was close, Tiff. Just keep practicing."

Tiffany smiled. "Want to see it again?"

"No," all three said in unison.

"There's Courtney," said Tiffany, ignoring the three older girls. "I need to go practice." She started pulling her skates out of her skate bag. "Shannon, help me get my skates on."

"Okay, Tiffany," said Shannon, "but you need to learn to lace up your own skates."

Why is everybody so crazy about Jamie? Shannon thought to herself while she helped her sister with her skates. *I'll bet Jamie isn't as good as she thinks she is. It's all her fault I can't practice jumps today.*

Shannon noticed Tiffany standing near the lobby door. "Go on, Tiff. What are you waiting for?"

"Nothing," said Tiffany, but she flashed a big grin at Shannon.

Shannon reached into her bag and pulled out her skates. Someone had undone the laces all the way to the end of her boots. She heard Tiffany giggle. "Tiffany!" yelled Shannon. But the joke was over and Tiffany had headed out for the rink.

Shannon knew it would take her a little longer to relace her skates. She did so very carefully, making sure she had plenty of support on her sore ankle. Then she went to the rink. She stepped on the ice and began stroking slowly around the rink to warm up her muscles. Gradually, she increased her speed, then began practicing crossovers. Fortunately, her ankle did not seem to hurt. Although it was tempting to try at least a waltz jump*, Shannon remembered her father's warning. It was important to let the injury heal properly or she would lose more practice time.

With Jamie on the ice, it wasn't easy to practice anyway. Whether Jamie was flying across the ice doing backward crossovers or landing double jump combinations directly in front of her, Shannon couldn't seem to stay out of her way. More than once, she was sure she saw a look of annoyance on Jamie's face when Shannon happened to get in her way. Shannon was glad when Jamie got off the ice only a half-hour after the session had started. *Now I can finally get something done,* she thought. She decided to work on spins.

After a few one-foot spins, Shannon's ankle began to hurt slightly, and she got off the ice to relace her skates. Looking around for her friends, she noticed that Amy and Kristen were no longer on the ice. *Where are they?* she wondered. *They never leave this early.* Shannon finished lacing her skates and stepped back on the ice, still searching for her friends.

Finally, she spotted them—in the lobby talking to Jamie. *They should be practicing,* Shannon thought, while she stroked around the ice. Faster and faster she skated, becoming more annoyed at her friends.

Shannon didn't realize how fast she was going until suddenly her feet flew out from under her and she slid halfway across the rink on her bottom.

Ouch! She could already feel the bruises. Realizing that people in the rink were watching her, she scrambled to her feet. Her cheeks burned with embarrassment. She didn't dare look toward the lobby; she was afraid her friends might have seen that humiliating fall.

"Are you all right?" Shannon looked up to see an Asian woman who looked about her mother's age. She was wearing figure skates and a green skating dress with a matching sweater.

Shannon smiled at her self-consciously. "Yes, I'm fine, thanks."

"You were skating with such wonderful speed," the woman said in a soft Korean accent.

Shannon laughed a little. "It was a fast slide, anyway!"

The woman smiled back. "A perfect fall. I should know! I am also very good at falling," she said, then winked at Shannon. "I don't believe we've met. I'm Carol Lee, and you are . . . ?"

"Shannon Roberts."

"It is very nice to meet you, Shannon Roberts," she said before she returned to her own skating.

Shannon watched her curiously for a few minutes as the woman performed a beautiful layback spin*. Shannon was amazed. She didn't know anyone that age could skate so beautifully.

Although she still felt a little shaky from her fall, Shannon went back to her own practice. At first she worried that the crash might have done more damage to her ankle. After all, her father had stressed that she not try any jumps. Fortunately, her ankle seemed to be okay, but maybe it was time to take a break.

❄ ❄ ❄ ❄ ❄

"Hi, Shannon."

Shannon turned to see Kristen step off the ice and sit down next to her. "Do you know Mrs. Lee?" Shannon asked, pointing toward the woman, who had just landed a beautiful single axel.

"Yes," Kristen said.

Shannon shook her head. "She's really good. I didn't know anybody that old could skate like that."

Kristen laughed. "Well, she's not like a hundred, you know. But she has been skating a long time. I've even seen her do double jumps."

"Wow!" Shannon was really impressed. "I thought only kids could do jumps and stuff."

"Lots of adults skate," said Kristen. "Usually, I've seen her here at night. She used to skate at my old rink in Richardson. I think she might have been a coach."

"Why?" asked Shannon.

"I don't know. I guess because sometimes she stops and teaches someone a new move. But mostly, she's pretty quiet," said Kristen.

This was something new for Shannon to think about. If Mrs. Lee could still do all those things at her age, surely there was plenty of time for her.

Shannon was more than ready to get off the ice an hour later when the session ended. She had her skates unlaced before Amy and Kristen quit practicing.

"Shannon, did you meet Jamie yet?" asked Amy as she sat down and pulled her shoes out of her skate bag.

"No." Shannon shook her head. "She left, didn't she?"

"Oh, I thought you might have had a chance before she left," said Amy. "Maybe we could introduce you? She's really cool. She promised to help me with my double lutz."

Shannon said nothing, but continued to put away her skates. Somehow she didn't think Jamie seemed like the helpful type.

Kristen appeared lost in thought. "Sometimes figure skating is kinda lonely."

"Yeah," said Amy. "We could ask her to do something with us. Maybe go to the mall next Saturday. What do you think?"

"She's probably too busy skating to go to the mall," said Shannon curtly.

"We could ask her anyway," suggested Amy.

"I don't know if I can go this Saturday," said Kristen.

"Well, I know I can't go," said Shannon. "Mom wants me to help with some housework." She didn't mention that her mother had chores for her every Saturday, but that they rarely took longer than an hour.

Shannon zipped her skate bag closed and stood up to leave. "We can do it another time."

"Well, I'll ask her. You guys figure out when you can go and let me know," Amy said.

❋ ❋ ❋ ❋ ❋

"How was skating?" asked Mrs. Roberts when she picked up the girls from the rink. "Is your ankle doing all right, Shannon?"

Before Shannon could open her mouth, Tiffany said, "That new girl was there again!"

"It isn't polite to interrupt, Tiffany," scolded her mother. "I asked Shannon a question. You should wait for her to answer. Now, Shannon, how's your ankle?"

"It didn't hurt at all," said Shannon.

"Now can I talk?" asked Tiffany. "Jamie's the bestest skater I've ever seen in my life!" She clapped her hands to her head for emphasis.

"Oh, really?" Their mother glanced in the rearview mirror toward Shannon, who was sitting in the back-seat. "Do you know anything about her, Shannon?"

Shannon looked out the window and answered casually, "She just moved here. She's training with

Coach Grischenko." She wasn't interested in saying much more, but her mother was full of curiosity.

"Did you get to meet her? Is she a good skater?"

"She's pretty good, I guess," answered Shannon without enthusiasm. "But I didn't meet her."

"Well, if she's new, it is up to you and your friends to make her feel welcome," said her mother. "Maybe you could invite her over one day."

Seated safely away from her mother's observation, Shannon rolled her eyes without answering.

"Can I invite her?" asked Tiffany. "Maybe she can come play with me."

"She didn't look like the kind that likes to play," said Shannon. That much was really true. Jamie seemed totally focused on her skating.

Tiffany folded her arms and looked over at Shannon. "I could show her all my stuffed animals. I have more animals than anyone in the world!"

"That's for sure!" mumbled Shannon.

As they turned into the driveway, Mrs. Roberts said, "Tiffany's got the right idea. You know, God tells us to be kind to strangers. You girls need to make an effort to be friends."

Shannon didn't say anything. She knew her mother was right. After all, she hadn't given Jamie much of a chance. Maybe she was nicer than she seemed.

Four

As the next week began, Shannon thought a lot about what her mother had said. She knew that God would want her to be friendly to Jamie, even if Jamie was a snob. Besides, she must feel pretty lonely living in a new town, skating in a new rink with a new coach.

Shannon couldn't imagine moving. She had lived in Walton as long as she could remember. Although she had been born in Korea, she couldn't remember anything about it. After all, her parents brought her home with them when she was only eight months old.

She was happy with her family here in Walton, Texas, and she couldn't imagine being anywhere else. *It would be hard to move away from my friends in Walton,* Shannon thought. *Maybe Jamie felt that way about Atlanta.* Shannon decided to invite Jamie to go to the mall Saturday, as Amy and Kristen had suggested. There was a new movie showing at the local theater, *Ice Queen.* Shannon couldn't wait to see it.

On Wednesday afternoon Shannon went to the rink with two plans. First, she was going to work hard on her skating; her father had finally given her permission to practice jumps. She usually had a lesson on Wednesday, but it was postponed to Friday. Shannon was glad because that would give her more time to practice before she talked to her coach about the competition. Second, she was going to make a sincere effort to make friends with Jamie.

Jamie wasn't on the ice when Shannon arrived, so she got right to work on her skating. After warming up, she decided to concentrate on the loop jump*. Although Shannon could land a good flip jump, which is usually considered more difficult, she always had a hard time with the loop jump.

She began setting up the jump, making a three-turn on her left foot, then shifting her weight onto the outside edge of her right blade. Traveling backward, she sprang into the air from her right foot and made a complete rotation in the air before landing backward on her right foot. Even though Shannon managed to land upright, her landing was not smooth. She knew she must be doing something wrong.

Perplexed, she stopped for a few moments. She tried to think about everything she had been taught about this jump. Finally, she tried it again. This time she completed the jump perfectly, landing on a smooth backward edge.

Shannon didn't need anyone to tell her she had gotten the jump right—it had been perfect. *No one could have done it better,* she thought. Then she heard an unfamiliar voice.

"You need more spring for that jump." It was Jamie, staring at her with big dark eyes.

Shannon's face turned red, more from annoyance than embarrassment. She paused. "Hey, I only learned this jump a few weeks ago."

"Well, I guess that was pretty good for a beginner," Jamie admitted.

Was that a compliment or an insult? Shannon was annoyed, but she remembered that she was making an effort to be friends with Jamie. She stifled her anger and smiled. "We haven't really met, have we? I'm Shannon."

Jamie gave a sort of half smile in return. "Hi. I'm Jamie. If you need any help with your skating, just ask. I've been skating practically all my life."

Shannon felt her good intentions evaporating. *What a braggart!* she thought. But all she said was, "Thanks, but I've got a great coach. I'm sure I won't need much help."

Jamie shrugged. "Well, nice meeting you."

Show-off. Shannon watched as Jamie's smooth, sweeping strokes took her across the ice. In spite of Jamie's attitude, it was impossible not to admire her skating. *Maybe that's why she's so stuck-up,* thought Shannon enviously. *If I was that good, I guess I'd be a little conceited, too.* Still, she was finding it hard to like Jamie.

Shannon was so busy watching Jamie out of the corner of her eye that she forgot to pay attention to her own skating. Whomp! Shannon felt herself ram into someone, and both skaters went tumbling onto the ice. To her utter embarrassment, it was Kevin!

"Sorry," she mumbled, mortified beyond words.

"*Sure* you are!" he teased, grinning at her. "I always knew you were out to get me!" Then to her surprise Kevin jumped to his feet and gallantly offered her his hand. "My Lady," he said as he took a deep bow.

Nervously, Shannon took his hand. "Thanks."

As soon as she was on her feet, Kevin smiled. Shannon thought he looked like he was starting to blush, but she would never know because he bowed again and dashed off to the other side of the rink.

❋ ❋ ❋ ❋ ❋

Later that day, Shannon noticed that Amy, Kristen, and Jamie were working together on jumps. Jamie seemed to be giving advice to them, too, but Amy and Kristen didn't appear to mind. They were listening intently.

I can't see what they see in her, thought Shannon resentfully. *They ought to be practicing.* She stroked idly around the rink as she watched her friends.

Shannon headed for the lobby shortly before the session was over. Amy and Kristen had spent almost the entire time with Jamie, but what really bothered Shannon was that her friends didn't even seem to notice they were ignoring her.

Amy and Kristen came into the lobby laughing and giggling at a story Jamie was telling them. "You should have seen her face!" laughed Jamie.

"Wow! Coach Grischenko would have never stood for that," said Kristen. "She'd kill us if we ever messed with the tape player."

"She was the coolest coach ever. She insisted we call her by her first name, Emily," said Jamie. "When she saw we had rigged the tape player to play rap music instead of the music for my routine, she laughed as hard as anybody. Of course, she told us never to do that again, but she wasn't really mad."

"I can't believe you left her to come here," said Amy. "I know Coach Grischenko is good, but you won novice regionals with Emily."

"I didn't want to move, but I didn't get a choice. My mom got a chance to transfer to a better job in this area," said Jamie, "and she had heard that Coach Grischenko was a really good coach for upper levels. So, here we are."

Shannon shifted uncomfortably on the bench nearby. She wished she could leave, but she had to wait for Tiffany. Shannon listened as the girls compared notes on coaches, training, and competitions.

"Hey, Jamie," said Kevin, joining the girls, "was that a triple lutz* you were working on?"

Jamie shrugged. "I give it a try sometimes." She acted like a triple lutz jump was an ordinary, everyday occurrence.

"Awesome!" said Kevin. "Maybe you could help Kristen with her double axel." He grinned wickedly at his sister. "Of course, I've already got mine!"

Amy and Kristen both turned to look at Kevin. Simultaneously, they said, "You can't land a—"

Kevin quickly interrupted them. "Really, Jamie, I've seen yours, and it's great."

"Well, I'll try to help," said Jamie. "But my double axel isn't all that good."

Give me a break, thought Shannon. *As if she doesn't know her double axel is perfect!* She thrust her skates into her bag and stood up. "Come on, Tiffany. It's time to go." She headed toward the door without looking back at her friends. Amy and Kristen didn't seem to even notice she was leaving.

Tiffany grabbed her skate bag and followed her, protesting, "But I wanted to ask Jamie to help me with my skating!"

Shannon gave a quick backward glance as they walked out the door. "You can talk to her next time, Tiff."

"You didn't even say good-bye," said Tiffany.

"I didn't want to interrupt," Shannon explained. "They won't mind." She had completely given up on the idea of making friends with Jamie.

More than ever, Shannon was sure she wanted to enter that competition. If Amy and Kristen could skate in this competition, so could she. She would show them—and Jamie, too!

Five

Shannon arrived early for ballet class on Thursday.

"Hi, Shannon," said Darcy, while she finished putting up her long brown hair. "Have you heard? Hannah's moving to California."

"But she has the solo part in the spring recital."

Darcy shrugged. "I guess Amanda will dance the part. She's the understudy."

I'm glad it's not me, thought Shannon. She had too much else to think about right now.

"I wish I could have the part," sighed Darcy. "I've always wanted a solo."

Darcy was tall, willowy, and a beautiful dancer. "I wish you could, too," said Shannon. "You're really good."

"Wouldn't you like the part?"

Shannon shook her head. "I'm kind of involved in my skating right now."

Darcy looked at her curiously. "You really like skating, don't you? Even more than dance."

Shannon hesitated. "I'm not sure," she said slowly.

The girls hurried into the studio, but all through class Shannon thought about what Darcy had said. Maybe she did like skating more than dance.

❄ ❅ ❆ ❅ ❄

Shannon was a little nervous waiting for her lesson on Friday afternoon. She had definitely decided to ask Coach Barnes if she could enter the big competition. Of course, she hadn't convinced her parents yet, but she was sure they would say yes—if she could get Coach Barnes to recommend that she go.

Shannon thought through her strategy while she went through her warmup routine. She needed to convince Coach Barnes that she should compete.

While Tiffany had her lesson, Shannon practiced every move she had learned. She needed to look as good as possible in order to show her coach she could handle the competition. She wondered what she would need to be able to do.

When it was finally time for her lesson, Shannon brought up the subject right off the bat. "Coach, Amy and Kristen told me there is a competition in Dallas in a few weeks. I would like to skate in it."

Her coach didn't answer at first. She gave Shannon a long, searching look while she thought over the question. Finally, she said, "Shannon, I wasn't planning for you to compete again so soon. This competition is much bigger than the last one. You've made wonderful progress in the last few months, but you need time to develop your skills."

"I know I can do it!" Shannon pleaded. "And it would push me to work harder."

Her coach still appeared unconvinced. "Most of the girls will have a lutz jump in their program, which you haven't even learned yet. They will also have a sit spin* and a camel spin*. We've worked on those, but they're certainly not ready to put in a program."

"Please. I'll work really, really hard."

Coach Barnes sighed deeply. "I'll consider it. In the meantime, let's see what you can do right now."

Well, a "maybe" is better than a "no," thought Shannon.

For the next half-hour her coach went over everything Shannon had learned since she began skating. By the time her lesson was over, Shannon felt as though she had run a marathon.

"You're doing well, Shannon," said her coach as she stepped off the ice. "I'm still not sure if I want you to take part in this competition, though. I'll decide later."

"I'll practice so hard I know you'll say 'yes,'" said Shannon.

Coach Barnes smiled and shook her head. "I don't think you have any idea what you're getting into."

Shannon didn't know what to say to that. Did she know what she was getting into?

"See you next time," said Coach Barnes. "Practice everything."

"I will." Shannon turned and headed back to the center of the rink. Usually, she took a break, but there was no time for that now. She had work to do.

There was only a half-hour of the session left, and Shannon used all of it. For once, she was the last skater to leave the ice when the Zamboni* came out to resurface at the end of the session.

Amy and Kristen were nearly ready to leave by the time Shannon joined them in the lobby, and Tiffany already had her skates in her bag, ready to go.

"I'm tired, Shannon," she complained. "Hurry up."

"Why are you in such a hurry?" teased Shannon. For once, Tiffany could wait on her. Shannon was in a good mood. She had had a great practice, and she felt sure her coach would let her compete.

"You were looking good today, Shannon," said Kristen while she stashed her skates in her bag.

"Thanks." Shannon glanced up briefly while she tugged at her skate laces. "I talked to my coach about the competition. She's thinking about letting me do it."

"Really?" Kristen seemed surprised. "Does she think you can have a program ready in time?"

"I guess I can do my *Star Wars* program from the last competition. I can just add some things."

Amy and Kristen exchanged glances. "Are you sure you want to do this competition, Shannon?" asked Amy. "There really isn't much time to get ready."

Shannon didn't understand her friends' reaction. She had expected them to be glad she was going to compete. She thought it would be fun to be together. *Could it be that they would rather hang around with Jamie?*

41

"I thought you would want me to compete," she said. "Last time you *wanted* me to compete."

"It's up to your coach," said Amy. "But this is a tough competition."

"Don't you think I can do it?" asked Shannon. She was feeling very hurt. *Didn't her friends believe in her?*

"It can be discouraging to go to a competition you aren't ready for," explained Kristen. "This is a big competition. It doesn't have a beginner level."

Shannon yanked at her remaining skate laces while she struggled to keep her composure. Clearly, her friends did not think she was good enough.

"Well, my coach thinks I can do it," said Shannon.

"Did she tell you that you could?" asked Amy.

Shannon hesitated. "Not exactly. She said she'll decide next week, but I think she's going to let me."

"If your coach says it's okay, you'll probably do okay," said Kristen. "I'll help you get ready."

"Me, too," said Amy.

"Thanks, guys," said Shannon, although she didn't feel very enthusiastic. Maybe Amy and Kristen thought the only reason she got a medal in the last competition was because they helped her so much. Maybe they didn't think she was a good skater at all.

Six

On Saturday morning Shannon almost wished she had gone through with her plan to invite her friends to a movie. Tiffany was spending the day with Courtney, but Shannon was home with nothing to do. She called Amy, then Kristen, but neither one was home.

After getting her mother's permission, Shannon called Darcy to invite her to go skating. At the rink, while she helped Darcy lace up her skates, Shannon remembered the first time she went skating and how her friends had helped her. It was fun to help someone else.

Darcy was a quick learner. Before long she was skating slowly alongside Shannon, only slightly unsteady. "Hey, this is fun!" she said. "I might try this again some time."

"Why don't you start coming all the time?" Shannon suggested. *It would be nice to have someone closer to my own level to skate with,* Shannon thought.

Darcy shook her head. "I'm too busy with dance. And besides," she added with a grin, "I'd be afraid I'd sprain my ankle!"

Shannon made a face. "You're never going to let me forget that, are you?"

"Maybe not," said Darcy. Then, as if on cue, her skates slid out from under her. As she fell she latched on to Shannon's arm and they both flew across the ice right into the boards . . . and Kevin!

Fortunately, no one was injured, but Shannon was flustered. Kevin smiled at her and said, "We've really got to stop meeting this way!" and he laughed. To her surprise, Shannon found herself laughing, too. Kevin sprinted off across the ice as Darcy turned to Shannon.

"He's cute," she said.

Shannon just nodded yes.

❊ ❊ ❊ ❊ ❊

Where are Amy and Kristen? Shannon wondered on Monday afternoon. The public session had started fifteen minutes ago. *They should have at least told me they were going to be late.*

Shannon had been working very hard, hoping to impress Coach Barnes with how well she was doing, and she was hoping Amy and Kristen could help her.

Shannon wondered if something was wrong. She had not seen either of her friends at school that day, but that was not unusual. Their schedules had changed when the new semester began. Now, Amy and Kristen had two classes together each day and had a different lunch period from Shannon's. She rarely saw either of them at school unless they made plans to meet.

"Shannon, watch me!" Tiffany demanded. "I learned a new jump!"

"Okay, Tiff." Shannon forced a smile. "Show me your new jump." She glanced once more toward the lobby, then turned to watch her little sister. Tiffany hopped from one skate blade to the other in an attempt at a bunny hop*, the first jump most kids usually learn. "Great job, Tiff," she said.

Tiffany beamed with pride. *I haven't given Tiffany much attention lately,* Shannon thought guiltily.

Tiffany usually spent more time playing around with her skating friends than practicing. However, she was doing amazingly well—in spite of all that.

"Am I as good as Jamie?" asked Tiffany when she finished. "I want to skate like her."

"Why Jamie?" asked Shannon. She was sick of hearing about how good Jamie was.

"'Cause Jamie's a champion!" replied the little girl. "She's the best skater in the whole world!"

"Okay, okay!" said Shannon. While her sister skated away, she glanced once more toward the empty lobby and decided Amy and Kristen weren't coming. She couldn't imagine why they would both take the day off unless they had something planned together. *I can't believe they didn't even let me know,* she thought.

Shannon took a deep breath and went to work on her own skating. She really missed having Amy and Kristen there to give advice. Before she knew it, the session was nearly over. Shannon stopped and looked at the clock mounted high above the Zamboni* room door. She was getting a little annoyed with her friends, who obviously weren't coming.

Shannon skated over to the side and reached for her skate guards. "Hi, Shannon!" She looked up to see Amy and Kristen stepping onto the ice.

"Where have you guys been?" Shannon couldn't help sounding a little annoyed.

Kristen looked at her very apologetically. "Coach Grischenko asked us to come later today. She wants to work with us during the evening freestyle sessions."

Freestyle sessions are private skating times reserved for figure skaters to practice their moves.

"Just for today, right?" asked Shannon.

Kristen hesitated before she answered. "Uh, no. I guess we're going to start skating late every day."

"Coach Grischenko wants to spend some extra time with us," explained Amy, "to get ready for this competition. And we need more space to do our programs."

"The public session is getting too crowded," added Kristen. "It isn't safe to practice our jumps anymore."

"Does that mean you won't be skating in the public sessions anymore?" Shannon felt deserted. It wasn't going to be nearly as much fun skating without her friends, and she was sure her parents would not agree to let her skate in the more expensive freestyle sessions.

"After the competition we will probably go back to our old schedule," Kristen said.

Just then Jamie showed up. "Hi, everyone."

"Jamie, have you met Shannon?" asked Amy.

"We've met," said Shannon.

"Hi, Shannon," said Jamie, smiling. "Hey, you guys, that was fun going to the mall last Saturday."

"The mall?" Shannon was stunned. Her friends went to the mall with Jamie, and they didn't invite her?

"Uh-huh," said Amy. "We all talked about it last Monday, but you said you couldn't go."

Shannon didn't know what to say. She *had* said she couldn't go, but she didn't think her friends would go without her. "My plans changed. I could have gone."

"I'm sorry, Shannon," said Kristen. "We thought we all agreed that you would call me if you could go."

Shannon was hurt. Even though she had told her friends she could not go with them, she did not remember that she was to call them. She felt they had purposely excluded her. There was an awkward silence. Amy and Kristen glanced at each other uneasily, while Jamie looked a little embarrassed.

"I have to get warmed up," Jamie said. "I've got a lesson in a little while." She took off around the rink.

Amy turned to Shannon. "There's still some time left. Did you want some help with anything?"

Shannon hesitated. She wasn't feeling much like skating right now, or even talking to her friends about the competition. "I've practiced enough for today," she said. She stepped off the ice and grabbed her skate guards. "I'll just wait for Tiff."

Amy and Kristen looked at each other and shrugged. "Okay. See you tomorrow."

Shannon knew her friends could tell she was angry, but right now she didn't care. It was their own fault. It was bad enough that they were deserting her for private sessions. They could have at least let her know they were taking Jamie to the mall. Shannon turned away from Amy and Kristen and headed for the lobby.

However, as she walked through the door, Shannon regretted the way she had just snubbed her friends. She started to turn around and go back out on the ice. But when she looked, she saw that the girls were already on the ice, laughing and talking together.

They don't even care, Shannon told herself. She sat down in the lobby and began pulling off her skates.

I guess they'd rather hang out with Jamie, she told herself. *I'm not good enough for them.*

For a moment, Shannon considered never coming back to the skating rink. But only for a moment. Even if she could never be as good at skating as Amy, Kristen, and Jamie, she knew she couldn't bear the thought of staying off the ice.

I'll show them, she thought. *Maybe one day they'll all be jealous of me.*

Seven

"All right, Shannon," said her coach at the beginning of her Wednesday lesson. "If you're really sure you want to enter this competition, let's go for it."

Shannon tried hard to suppress a big grin. She didn't want to appear too excited. "I'm sure," she said.

"Is it okay with your parents?" her coach asked.

Shannon hesitated. "Well, I haven't mentioned it lately, but I know it will be all right." It wouldn't do to tell her coach that she hadn't talked to her parents about it. She would just have to convince them.

Coach Barnes looked suspicious. "There are some entry forms in the coaches' room. Remind me to give you one before you go home today. The deadline is Friday. Of course, there is a fee."

Shannon nodded.

"Very well, then. We have our work cut out for us. Do you have the tape from your last program with you?"

"Yes," she said.

"Good. Let's run through the whole program."

The coach put the tape on, and the familiar music from *Star Wars* filled the arena. Shannon would have liked to have chosen new music for this competition, but she knew there was not enough time to make a new tape and plan a completely new program. As she began going through the familiar choreography*, she tried to complete every move as perfectly as she could, but she was still wobbly on some of the moves. When the music ended, she was afraid to look at her coach, expecting to see a frown of disapproval.

However, Coach Barnes just said, "Okay, Shannon, we're going to have to make some major changes. You need more jumps. We're going to add a flip and a loop jump. And we really need to put in a sit spin."

For the next half-hour, Shannon's coach worked with her on her program, changing a jump here, adding a jump there. She had Shannon do sit spins until her legs were sore from squatting, and her bottom was sore from falling.

Shannon brushed the ice off her tights and took a deep breath. She was tired and ready to take a break.

Her coach must have read her thoughts. "Shannon, if you choose to enter this competition, you're going to have to work very hard—harder than you have ever worked on anything. Are you sure you're up to it?"

Shannon nodded, but inside she wasn't quite as sure.

"Well, if you're willing to work so hard, so am I," her coach said. "Let's start again."

At the end of her lesson, Shannon was exhausted. She hadn't expected so many changes in her program. This was starting to sound like a lot of work, but Shannon was determined to enter the competition. She had managed to convince her coach, and she didn't want to back down now. All she had to do was convince her parents.

❆ ❆ ❆ ❆ ❆

At supper, Shannon looked for the opportunity to bring up the subject.

Tiffany was the first to mention skating. "I learned a new jump today," she said.

"What new jump did you learn?" asked her mother.

Tiffany wrinkled her nose, crumpling her napkin while she thought. "I don't remember," she said.

"A ballet jump*," provided Shannon.

Tiffany nodded. "Yeah, a ballet jump. And Coach Barnes said I did great in my lesson."

Mrs. Roberts smiled approvingly. "I can't wait to come watch. You should see her, Jim. She's getting to be a wonderful little skater."

Shannon picked at her food, annoyed that Tiffany always seemed to be the center of interest. "Would anybody like to hear how my lesson was?" she asked.

"I would love to hear," said her dad.

"Well, Coach Barnes started teaching me the lutz. It's the hardest single jump next to the axel."

"Sounds super," said her father.

"Well, I don't quite have it yet," she admitted. "But I need to get it in time for the next big competition."

"Oh, when is that?" asked Mrs. Roberts.

"The third week of March. It's the one in Dallas I was telling you about. My coach sent home an entry form."

"Hmm." Mrs. Roberts looked at Shannon searchingly. "I thought we settled this—"

"Mom, you didn't say no, you said maybe."

"You just competed. Are you sure you can get ready for another competition so soon?" asked Mrs. Roberts.

Shannon nodded. "Coach Barnes said I could use my *Star Wars* program, if we added some things. And I could practice a lot."

"A lot? What does that mean?" asked her father.

"I could practice in the mornings before school, in the afternoons, and in the evenings. I could take extra lessons, too," said Shannon eagerly.

"Does the coach want Tiffany to enter?"

Shannon shook her head. "I don't think so. This is a competition for *higher level* skaters."

"That isn't fair," complained Tiffany. "If Shannon's competing, I want to!"

Shannon ignored her sister and looked at her parents. Mr. and Mrs. Roberts quickly exchanged glances. "Please," begged Shannon.

Finally, her father spoke. "Your mother and I will discuss this later."

This is not good, Shannon thought. Her heart sank as she realized they might not give their permission, but she didn't argue.

"Bet you can't go!" whispered Tiffany. She stuck out her tongue at her sister when her parents weren't looking. Shannon glared at her.

❋ ❋ ❋ ❋ ❋

Shannon was working on homework when her mother came into her room to talk to her. "Shannon, your father and I have discussed this. If your coach has given you permission to enter this competition, we have decided to allow you to enter. But only under the following conditions . . ."

Shannon listened intently to her mother.

"You must keep your grades up in school—"

"I can do that," interrupted Shannon.

Her mother gave her a stern look that Shannon knew meant she shouldn't have interrupted. "You must keep up with your ballet, or you'll have to drop out of the competition. Do you understand this agreement?"

"Yes," said Shannon.

"Are you sure you want to do this?" asked her mother.

"I'm sure."

Shannon was happy her parents had given their okay. Now, if she could just get rid of the butterflies fluttering around in her stomach whenever she thought about competing.

❋ ❋ ❋ ❋ ❋

After supper, the phone rang. It was Amy.

"Shannon, I didn't get a chance to talk to you today. Did your coach say you can do the competition?"

"Yes! We are already working on my program!" Shannon carried the cordless phone into her room and lounged on her bed while she talked.

"Well, I'll be glad to help."

"Thanks." Shannon was glad Amy had made the offer. Maybe her friends did care about her a little. At least one of her friends. "I'm getting a little nervous. I didn't realize how difficult my program was going to be. My coach wants me to have a sit spin, a flip jump, and maybe even a lutz. I haven't even learned the lutz yet!"

"Whoa!" Amy sounded sympathetic. "Well, don't worry. You still have a few weeks to get them. If you don't, Coach Barnes will probably take them out."

"If I don't have them in my program, I won't win. Will I?"

Amy hesitated before answering. "It depends on who's competing, and on how well you do the other stuff in your program."

"Oh." Shannon was really beginning to feel unsure of herself.

"You'll be okay."

"Yeah, I guess so." Shannon was definitely starting to wonder what she had gotten herself into.

"Well, I gotta go," said Amy. "I'll see you tomorrow at the rink. Oh, wait—you've got ballet class tomorrow, don't you? Well, I'll see you on Friday then. By the way, Jamie invited us to come over to her house on Friday night to watch a movie. She said she wants you to come, too, if you can. Do you think you could?"

"Um, I don't think my mom will let me. She has this rule about not visiting people she doesn't know." Shannon wondered if inviting her had truly been Jamie's idea, but she was glad to have a good excuse not to go.

"Oh. Hey, maybe she could meet Jamie and her mom on Friday," offered Amy.

"Her mom never comes to the rink," said Shannon.

"Well, Friday she's supposed to meet with the coach," said Amy.

"Um . . . I don't think that would work."

"Oh." Amy sounded disappointed.

"Bye, Amy." Shannon hung up the phone, feeling guilty. She knew her mother would have been glad to meet both Jamie and her mom. After all, it was her mother's suggestion that they reach out to Jamie. Not only had Shannon made no effort to be friends, but she was in danger of losing the friends she already had.

Buttons hopped up on the bed. Shannon reached out and rubbed his ears. She was comforted by the loud purring sound he made.

Suddenly, the competition didn't seem quite as important.

Eight

"Shannon, are you paying attention?" Mr. Terino stopped in the middle of his lecture on the digestion of carbohydrates. To Shannon's horror he was staring straight at her.

"I'm sorry, Mr. Terino." She could feel her face burning. Quickly, she picked up her pencil and tried to look as though her full attention was focused on her science teacher and the diagram of the digestive system on the overhead projector.

However, try as she might, Shannon found it almost impossible to keep her mind on her notes. *Mr. Terino must be the most boring teacher alive,* she thought. But the truth was that even the most fascinating teacher on earth would have had trouble getting her attention today.

Shannon couldn't stop thinking about the competition and all the work she needed to do to get ready. She chewed the end of her pencil as she considered the problem.

Even if she worked very hard, she wasn't sure she could get those moves down perfectly, especially since she only had three days a week to practice. Yet she knew that if she couldn't perform everything the other girls were doing, she wouldn't have a chance at winning a medal.

Shannon bit the end off the eraser. The answer was simple. She needed more practice time. If she could skate five days a week, she was sure she could get her program ready in time.

Because of ballet class, she couldn't skate on Tuesday and Thursday afternoons. Was there another time she could practice? Shannon doodled on her notes while she thought of the possibilities. Would her parents allow her to skate in the evening freestyles after ballet class? Shannon didn't think so, because freestyle sessions cost more than public sessions.

She thought about skating in the public session at night, but that wouldn't work either. Those sessions were always very crowded. Besides, they ended at ten o'clock, and her parents would never allow her to stay out so late on a school night.

Shannon could see only one way to get more practice: She would somehow have to get out of going to ballet class. But how?

Suddenly, Mr. Terino interrupted her thoughts. "Would you like to tell us where you've been, Shannon?" Several of the kids snickered while the science teacher stared straight at her. "You obviously haven't been here with us."

Shannon was too embarrassed to speak. She was grateful when the bell rang a few moments later and she could gather her books and escape.

✳ ✳ ✳ ✳ ✳

There was no way to cut ballet class Thursday afternoon, so it was Friday before Shannon could get back to the rink. She lost no time in getting her skates on; she needed every minute on the ice.

Once she was there, however, she found it hard to practice. Skating by herself was boring. She missed having Amy and Kristen to practice with. Even Kevin was skating in the freestyles. Although Shannon hated to admit it, she missed Kevin's antics.

She wondered if Amy would come early today. After all, she had promised to help her get her program ready. Shannon watched the lobby for a few minutes, but when she saw no sign of her friend, she decided to work on her own. *Amy probably forgot,* thought Shannon.

She worked on sit spins until her legs were sore, but she couldn't tell whether she was making any improvement. She knew that when she bent low to the ice her free leg should be turned out and extended and her back should be straight. If only Amy and Kristen were here. They could always tell her what she was doing wrong and how to do it right.

Shannon took a short break and then started working on her lutz jump. Her coach had worked with her on it for a short while during her last lesson, but Shannon had not succeeded in landing it during her lesson.

Oh, well, here goes nothing. Shannon skated backward into the corner of the rink on a left outside edge. Reaching back, she jabbed her right toe pick into the ice, simultaneously springing from her left blade. However, she had only made a half turn in the air before she came down on both feet.

Over and over, Shannon attempted the jump with the same result each time. After several tries, she began to get frustrated. Every time she failed the jump, she grew more and more angry until at last she kicked at the ice with her blade.

"We don't need any more holes in the ice!"

Shannon turned, embarrassed at having lost her temper. It was Mrs. Lee, the adult skater she had seen a few weeks earlier.

"I know the lutz is difficult, but more holes will not help," Mrs. Lee said.

"I'm sorry." Shannon felt her face turning red. "It's just that I've tried so hard, and I still can't do this jump."

"Why don't you try again, and I will watch. Maybe I can see what you are doing wrong."

Shannon remembered Mrs. Lee's beautiful layback spin. Maybe she really could help. She obeyed and tried the jump once more—with the same result as before. Upset, she looked at Mrs. Lee.

"I think I see. Here, try it this way." Mrs. Lee demonstrated how to do a lutz, step by step. When she finished, Shannon said, "Let me try again."

This time when Shannon jumped, she completed almost the full turn before landing on both feet.

"Yes, that was better!" said Mrs. Lee enthusiastically. "That time you made the full rotation. But now you must learn to land on one foot."

Shannon nodded. "I see. Now I just have to do it!"

"You will have the lutz very soon, I am sure."

"Thank you for helping me," said Shannon gratefully. "And I'm sorry I kicked the ice."

Mrs. Lee laughed. "I get angry myself sometimes."

Shannon thought Mrs. Lee was really nice. She wondered how long she had been skating and why she still practiced so hard. After all, she was too old to go to the Olympics or anything like that.

Shannon practiced the lutz jump a few more times before getting off the ice. She was disappointed that Amy had never shown up, but at least Mrs. Lee had helped her learn the lutz jump.

Tiffany was still playing around on the ice with one of her friends when Shannon went on into the lobby and sat down in a corner. Bending down to unlace her skates, she heard voices speaking in a whisper, "Do you think she'll be surprised?"

Although Shannon could not see who was speaking, she recognized Amy's voice. Since she was sitting behind a partition, she realized that Amy did not know she was there.

"I'll talk to her mom and make sure she'll be there." That was Kristen. But what were they talking about, and who were they planning to surprise?

Amy giggled. "I can't wait to see her face. She'll just die!"

"Yeah, I bet she won't believe we know when her birthday is."

Shannon grinned to herself. So that was it. Her thirteenth birthday was coming up in just a few weeks, and her friends were planning a surprise party for her. She retreated farther back into the corner, hoping they wouldn't discover her presence. She wouldn't want to ruin their plans.

"Shhh. Here comes Jamie," Kristen whispered. "We'll talk about this later."

Jamie? The smile faded from Shannon's face. The surprise party her friends were planning must be for *Jamie!*

Shannon didn't move. She didn't want her friends to know she was there, so she waited until they were gone. She was hurt that they were planning a party for Jamie, whom they had just met. *How could they have a party for Jamie, when it's my birthday, too? And they didn't even invite me to the party,* thought Shannon.

Nine

Shannon decided the only way to have time for more skating practice was to skip ballet class. She didn't really want to quit entirely, but right now it seemed more important to practice for the skating competition.

Of course, her parents would be furious if they found out, but what else could she do? And how could she keep Tiffany from telling their parents?

Fortunately, the ice rink was only a couple of blocks from the ballet studio. Shannon came up with a plan: She would pack her skates and her clothes in her ballet bag. Once she got to the ballet class, she could sneak out to the rink. Tiffany had been invited to a skating party on Tuesday afternoon, so her mother had asked if Shannon was willing to get Tiffany and meet her outside the rink after her class. Shannon had just enough money saved to pay for the skating session.

Shannon felt terrible about deceiving her parents. She knew it was wrong, but she just had to have more practice. If she was going to skate well at the competition, she would have to convince her parents that she needed more practice time. Then perhaps she could skate in the freestyle sessions before school. That way she could still keep up with her ballet class on Tuesday and Thursday afternoons.

How to keep Tiffany from squealing was a bigger problem. Tiffany had been invited to that party. Since she would be at the rink, Shannon would just have to include her in the plan and trust her to keep the secret. Shannon's only hope was to make Tiffany understand how important it was for her to practice for the competition.

❄ ❄ ❄ ❄ ❄

"You're going to skip ballet?" Tiffany asked in horror when Shannon tried to explain. "And you're not going to tell Mommy?"

"It can't be helped," said Shannon impatiently. "The competition is in three weeks. If I don't get more practice, I'll never be ready in time."

Tiffany frowned and shook her head. "Mommy and Daddy will be really mad when they find out."

"Never mind. Just don't tell, okay?"

Tiffany stuck out her lower lip and folded her arms defiantly.

"Please, Tiff. This is really important. I promise I'll tell them myself after the competition."

Tiffany thought for a minute. "Will you teach me a toe loop? Courtney can already do one."

Shannon shook her head. "You need to wait for Coach Barnes to teach you that."

"Then I'm going to tell." Tiffany turned around and headed toward the kitchen, where her mother was fixing dinner.

Shannon gave in. "Okay, okay, but not a toe loop. I'll teach you a waltz jump."

Tiffany turned back, smiling victoriously. "Okay, I won't tell," she agreed.

Shannon knew Tiffany was right, but she could think of no other solution. She just had to have more practice.

On Tuesday afternoon, Shannon was ready. She packed her ballet bag with her skates and clothes.

"What are you working on in your ballet class today?" asked her mother as she drove her to the studio.

"Oh, the same old things, I guess," said Shannon evasively. She suddenly felt very guilty about what she had planned. For a few minutes, she thought about backing out of her scheme, but then she remembered she hadn't brought her ballet clothes and slippers. It would never do to show up at Madame Junot's without her things. There was nothing to do but go through with the whole plan.

"When are we supposed to have the money in for your recital costumes?"

Shannon had forgotten about the recital costumes. They were supposed to be measured and ordered on Thursday afternoon.

"Shannon?"

Shannon jerked back to reality. "On Thursday," she answered.

"Remind me to send a check with you."

"Sure, Mom." This wasn't going to be easy.

When they got to the studio, Shannon grabbed her bag and climbed out of the car as quickly as she could. It was a good thing the ballet studio was in the back of the building or Madame Junot would surely see her. Still, she needed to get out of sight as quickly as possible.

She walked into the building and into the ladies' rest room on the first floor. Then she looked at her watch. After waiting until ballet class had started, she slipped out of the building and hurried down the street as fast as she could go. By the time she reached the rink, she was out of breath.

Tiffany was already on the ice, playing with a couple of her friends, when Shannon arrived.

Shannon turned to see her coach walking through the lobby with a cup of coffee. "Shannon! I didn't expect to see you here this afternoon," said her coach. "I thought you had ballet class today."

Shannon gulped. "Uh, I . . . uh, the class was canceled for today . . ."

"So you decided to get in some extra practice. Great!" She took a sip of her coffee, pulled her coat around her, and walked back into the rink.

Shannon hadn't expected to find herself lying to everyone. By the time she got on the ice, she realized she had made a big mistake, but it was too late to turn back. She was already there, she might as well skate.

After spending a few minutes attempting to teach Tiffany a waltz jump, Shannon wasted no time getting to work. As soon as she had warmed up, she began working on her sit spin. Skating backward crossovers, she held a long inside edge on her right foot, making a circular pattern on the ice. Stepping into the circle with her left foot, she immediately lowered herself into a "sitting" position, bending her left knee as deeply as she could while extending her right foot in front. *One . . . two . . . three . . . four . . .* she counted her revolutions. Shannon knew that the judges would be counting the number of turns she made in her spin. It was important to make at least four revolutions in the spin. Shannon straightened her leg and finished with an upright one-foot spin.

My sit spin is getting better, she thought happily. *Now, for the lutz jump.*

Shannon took a deep breath. This was harder, and she was less sure of herself, although Mrs. Lee had helped her a lot. Shannon looked around to see if her friend was at the rink this afternoon, but she didn't see her anywhere.

She skated backward into the corner of the rink on the outside edge of her left blade to set up the jump. Giving a quick look back, she checked to be sure no one was in the way. Then, with her left arm extended forward and her right arm backward, she reached behind with her right foot, jabbed her toe pick into the ice, and vaulted into the air. She pulled her arms in to help with the rotation, but she hadn't completed a full turn before she came down sideways and fell.

Exasperated, Shannon sat on the ice for a few seconds, trying to figure out what she was doing wrong. She couldn't believe she was having so much trouble learning this jump—especially after learning the others so quickly. And she knew that unless she had it down Coach Barnes would never allow her to use it in her program.

Shannon tried the jump several more times, without success. The session was almost over, and she still had not landed it. She decided to go through her entire program, from start to finish, but without the lutz.

Shannon first went through the entire program without her music. She wanted to concentrate on getting all the moves right. Starting with her first jump, a waltz jump–toe loop jump* combination, things went fairly smoothly. One by one, she completed each move. One-foot spin. Flip jump. Loop jump. Spiral*. Salchow. Her final move, a sit spin, went well, although she didn't complete all four revolutions.

Shannon stepped off the ice for a short break, grabbing her water bottle. If she could leave out the lutz, she felt pretty good about the rest.

"Hi, Shannon." Shannon turned to see Jamie getting ready to step on the ice. Jamie reached down and pulled off a skate guard.

"Oh. Hi, Jamie." Shannon remembered she was supposed to be friendly.

"Nice program," said Jamie. "What music are you skating to?"

"*Star Wars*. I'm going to do a run-through with music in a few minutes."

Jamie nodded. "How long have you been skating?"

"Just since last September."

"You're pretty good, considering you haven't been skating long." Jamie lined up her skate guards in a spot near the entrance to the ice. "It's too bad you didn't start earlier. You could have been a really good skater if you had started when you were five or six."

Shannon was so stunned her mouth almost dropped open. *What did Jamie mean by that comment, anyway?* "I never had the chance to skate until the rink opened. I started as soon as I could," she said defensively.

Jamie shrugged. "Sorry. I didn't mean anything by it—it's just too bad that you didn't start training early enough to be a top skater."

Shannon was annoyed. "How do you know I can't be a top skater?"

Jamie shrugged. "It's just that top skaters start skating when they're very young."

"Well, you never know." Shannon tried to sound indifferent, even though Jamie's remarks had hurt. "I guess I'll just try to be as good as I can." She turned and reached for her skate bag. There was no way she was going to run through her program now—not with Jamie on the ice.

"Hey, I'm sorry," said Jamie. "I really didn't think I was telling you anything you didn't already know. Lots of people compete just for fun, you know." She stepped on the ice and immediately began stroking at high speed around the rink, warming up.

Shannon picked up her things and headed back into the lobby. Of course, many of the champion skaters did begin their training when they were very small, but a few broke from tradition and learned to skate later. And she'd had ballet training.

Still, Jamie's remarks had hurt. But Shannon didn't see why she couldn't be a wonderful skater if she worked hard. But then, if she truly didn't have a chance to become a top skater, why was she working so hard?

This was a disaster, thought Shannon while she changed out of her skating clothes. She wished she hadn't skipped ballet class. Coming to the rink today had been a big mistake. She had learned her lesson. *Dear God, forgive me for lying and making a mess of things.*

Ten

Shannon checked her watch. Science class would be over in a few minutes, and she could hardly wait. Mr. Terino's lecture seemed to go on and on. Shannon had always loved science until this year. Somehow Mr. Terino made it seem so difficult. Shifting in her chair, she listened carefully while the teacher gave the homework assignment for that evening.

Shannon sighed as she closed her notebook. Although she was keeping up with the homework, she felt as though she was getting farther and farther behind. It was a relief when the bell finally rang to signal the end of class.

After what happened at the rink yesterday, Shannon didn't have her mind on school anyway. She felt guilty about deceiving her parents and confused by what Jamie had said.

Walking through the hall to her locker, she was surprised to see Amy and Kristen waiting for her.

"Hello, stranger," said Amy.

"We've hardly talked to you in ages," said Kristen, "not even at the rink. So we decided to corner you."

"Yeah," added Amy. "It's too bad we don't have the same lunch period anymore."

Shannon didn't know what to say. She wondered why Amy and Kristen went out of their way to see her. She thought they didn't care about her anymore.

"I guess I've been kind of busy," mumbled Shannon, juggling her books while she dialed her locker combination. "I'm working hard to get ready for this competition."

"Too busy for us?" asked Amy playfully. "I guess you're getting so good you don't need our expert coaching anymore."

Shannon smiled a little. "Actually, I need all the help I can get. I even got Mrs. Lee to help me with my lutz."

Kristen poked Amy. "So that's the problem. She's found a better coach!"

Shannon looked up quickly. "Oh, no. I mean, Mrs. Lee is very nice, but she's not a great skater or anything. She's not nearly as advanced as you guys."

Kristen shook her head. "Don't underestimate Mrs. Lee. She may not be doing many double jumps, but she's been skating for a long time. She's really good."

Shannon felt confused. "But she's not like you guys. She couldn't go to the Olympics or anything."

Kristen shrugged. "So? A lot of good skaters don't make it to the Olympics. You know, Mrs. Lee has won a lot of adult competitions."

Shannon had never thought about adults competing. "Anyway, she did help me with my lutz."

"I wish we could help, too," said Amy. "We need to get together. What if I get my homework done fast tonight and meet you at the rink."

Shannon wondered if Amy meant what she said. "Okay. But I have a lesson with Coach Barnes today."

"Oops, there goes the first bell," said Kristen. "I'd better get to my next class. I need to check over my homework before I hand it in."

"Me, too," said Amy. "See you tonight, hopefully."

Shannon stuffed her science book into her locker and pushed the pile of other stuff aside to find the literature book for her next class. She was glad Amy and Kristen had come to see her, but she was a bit suspicious. What were they up to? Maybe they just wanted to invite her to Jamie's surprise party.

After what happened yesterday, the last thing she wanted to do was go to a surprise party for Jamie. Shannon guessed she would have to go if they invited her. As much as she disliked Jamie, she knew God— and her mom—would want her to do the right thing. And the right thing was to be nice to Jamie.

❋ ❋ ❋ ❋ ❋

The coach wasted no time that afternoon. "Let's get right to work," she said at the beginning of Shannon's lesson. She had Shannon perform every element in her program as she critiqued each move.

Shannon still couldn't land the lutz and was relieved when her coach took it out of her program. She had enough things to worry about. The coach put on the familiar music of *Star Wars,* and Shannon began to skate, trying to remember everything she had learned.

At first things went well. The waltz jump–toe loop jump combination was perfect. The one-foot spin was next, and Shannon performed it without a hitch. But by the time she got to the loop jump, she began to struggle to keep up with the music. Although Shannon could do every move by itself, it was harder to do them in a timed sequence. When she came to the slower section of the program, there was barely time to do her spiral. She cut it short, but she was still behind the music. Rushing to catch up, she tripped on her toe pick and fell flat on her face.

Coach Barnes called to her from the side: "Don't stop! Finish the program!"

Shannon picked herself up as quickly as she could, ignoring the bump she could already feel on her knee, and hurried to do the salchow jump*. By the time she went into her final move, the sit spin, the music had already stopped. Shannon completed the spin anyway and struck her final ending pose, but she was angry with herself. She knew she had skated terribly, and there were only a couple of weeks left until the competition!

Coach Barnes waited for her by the boards. "Shannon, are you sure you want to do this competition?"

Shannon nodded, although at the moment she wasn't sure of anything.

Her coach stared at her for a long moment. "You're just not ready yet, Shannon. Why don't we skip this one? I know you'll be ready for the next one."

"I know I can do it. I've still got a couple of weeks," Shannon pleaded.

Coach Barnes sighed. "Even if we work really hard . . ." She paused and looked hard at Shannon. "I'm afraid you may be disappointed in your performance."

For just a moment, Shannon hesitated. She wasn't sure why she had to enter this competition; she only knew she had to. She stared at her coach with large dark eyes. "I know. I'm willing to take that chance."

"All right. I want to see you working as hard as you can between now and your next lesson. I'll be watching." Coach Barnes turned to look for her next student.

Shannon didn't even take a break. She was determined to show her coach that she could get ready for this competition. And if she worked hard enough, maybe she could even win a medal. Then maybe Coach Barnes would believe in her.

And maybe she could believe in herself.

❄ ❄ ❄ ❄ ❄

The session was almost over before Shannon remembered that Amy had promised to try to come early to help her with her program. She looked up at the clock, which showed only five minutes left. Then she looked toward the lobby to see if she could see Amy or Kristen—or even Jamie; but she didn't see any of them.

I knew she wouldn't really come, Shannon thought. She told herself that she didn't care, but inside she knew that she was disappointed. Finally, she saw Amy, Kristen, and Jamie coming into the lobby, laughing and talking together. They looked as if they had just arrived.

Shannon started stroking around the rink as fast as she could. She was determined to look as if she didn't care whether they were there or not.

"Shannon!" She turned to see Amy standing by the ice, waving to her. Shannon reluctantly skated to her.

"I'm sorry I couldn't come earlier," Amy explained. "Mrs. Powell assigned us a major project for history class tomorrow."

Shannon tried to look indifferent. "That's okay. I had a lesson today anyway."

"I could come early Friday," Amy said.

Shannon shrugged. "Okay."

Amy didn't seem to notice Shannon's lack of enthusiasm. "I'll see you Friday then. I'd better hurry and get my skates on." She turned and rushed back into the lobby.

Shannon stepped off the ice with mixed feelings. *If Amy really wanted to help, she would have been here,* she thought.

Eleven

Shannon didn't dare miss ballet class again the same week, especially since today was the day for ordering recital costumes. She arrived early for class, but before she could get into her practice shoes, her friend Darcy stopped her.

"Where were you on Tuesday?" whispered Darcy.

Shannon answered vaguely. "Something came up."

"I guess you missed the announcement."

"What announcement?"

"Madame Junot announced that they're choosing someone from this class to dance a solo in the spring recital." Darcy reached up to pin her long hair in a tight knot.

Shannon looked confused. "I thought Amanda was dancing that part. She was Hannah's understudy."

"Didn't you hear? She broke her leg Rollerblading. I think it'll be Tammy," whispered Darcy as the girls walked into the rehearsal room.

"As long as it's not me," said Shannon. "I'm too busy. I'm compet—"

"Here comes Madame," interrupted Darcy.

Shannon hurried into position. Madame Junot's classes were very formal. Her students were expected to greet her properly when she walked in and perform a révérence, a type of choreographed curtsey, at the end of the class.

Madame Junot was tall and thin with piercing blue eyes and a sharp nose. She wore her dark gray-streaked hair in a tight bun.

"Good afternoon, girls." Madame took her place quickly. "Shannon, we missed you on Tuesday."

Shannon mumbled something about not being up to dancing that day. Madame lifted an eyebrow, but said nothing more about the missed class.

It was obvious that Madame had something important to tell them. "The spring recital is not far away, and there is much to do to prepare. First, our new soloist will be Shannon Roberts. Shannon, you will stay after class, and I will speak with you about the special rehearsals." She paused a moment, her eyes scanning the class. "Now, I also have to fill Shannon's role. I will hold auditions after class Tuesday."

Madame clapped her hands and the students obediently took their positions at the barre. "Now, class . . ."

Shannon was in shock. Darcy shot her a look of annoyance, but Shannon hardly noticed. To be chosen without an audition for an important solo part was an honor. A few weeks ago, Shannon would have been thrilled. Now, however, all she could think about was what this would do to her skating and her preparations for the competition. For a few minutes, it was all Shannon could do to keep up with the exercises.

"Shannon!" Madame's sharp rebuke startled her out of her thoughts. "Pay attention to what you're doing."

For the rest of the hour, Shannon focused as well as she could on ballet class. Finally, class was over, and Shannon was alone with Madame.

Madame turned and gave her a rare smile. "You have done well, Shannon. In spite of your inattention today." She made a slight frown. "But I guess you were excited about the solo." She handed Shannon a sheet of paper. "Here are the rehearsal times. I will also need to work with you by yourself to teach you the part."

Madame started to turn to go and then added, "I would like to see you devote yourself more seriously to your dancing. That's why you were chosen."

"Thank you." Shannon didn't know what to say. How could she possibly tell Madame Junot that she didn't want the solo? It was unthinkable. She looked at the rehearsal times, They were all in the afternoon! Four o'clock. Right in the middle of the afternoon skating session. Slowly, Shannon realized what this meant. *Now I have a real problem!*

Twelve

"Did you get the money in for the recital costume?" asked Mrs. Roberts, while she worked on supper that evening and Shannon set the table.

Shannon was so busy thinking about the problem of recital practices that she didn't even hear her mother.

"Shannon?" Mrs. Roberts stopped in the middle of scrubbing carrots and looked straight at her daughter.

Shannon was startled back to reality. "Um . . . yes." Then, for the first time, Shannon realized she would not be wearing the same costume as the rest of the class. She wondered what her costume would look like and if it would be pretty.

"Shannon, are you all right?" asked her mother, putting down the scrub brush and walking over to look at Shannon.

"Why, yes . . . I'm fine, Mom."

Mrs. Roberts appeared unconvinced. "You seem preoccupied. Did something happen?"

How does she always know? Shannon wondered. "Uh, well, I have some good news and some bad news."

Her mother waited for Shannon to continue.

"Madame Junot wants me to dance a solo part in the spring ballet recital."

"Shannon, that's wonderful!" said her mother. "So what's the problem?"

Shannon hesitated. She wasn't sure her mother would understand. "She gave me a list of the practices. They're all in the afternoon at four o'clock."

Mrs. Roberts looked puzzled. "That's the same time as ballet class, isn't it?"

Shannon shook her head. "You don't understand. The rehearsals are on Mondays and Wednesdays. That's right in the middle of skating."

A look of understanding dawned on her mother's face. "I see."

"Mom, I can't miss skating practice, especially now, with the competition coming up."

Mrs. Roberts sat down at the kitchen table, drying her hands on a dishtowel. "Shannon, you know what an honor it is to be chosen for a solo in the recital. Maybe you should forget about this competition. I wasn't in favor of you doing this one anyway."

"But I've already paid and signed up and everything!" said Shannon.

"I'm not concerned about the money, Shannon. But you have worked hard to be a soloist," said her mother.

"Why don't you want me to skate?" asked Shannon in exasperation. "All you care about is Tiffany's skating!"

"That's not true, Shannon, and you know it." Her mother's voice was stern.

"It *is* true! You always think Tiffany is so cute, and you buy her new skating dresses and everything. You won't even listen when I tell you how important skating is to me." Shannon fought back tears. "I have to practice for the competition. If I have to quit ballet to do it, I will." She turned and fled from the room, slamming the door as she went. *Why couldn't her parents understand how much skating meant to her?*

❋ ❋ ❋ ❋ ❋

Alone in her room, Shannon felt guilty about talking that way to her mother. She flung herself down on her bed and buried her face in a pillow. Why did everything have to get so complicated when all she wanted to do was skate? Madame Junot would never tolerate her missing rehearsals. And she was sure her mother would insist she drop out of the competition rather than the recital.

Shannon didn't know what to do. She had to admit it would be cool to have a solo in the recital—she couldn't believe Madame Junot had chosen her. Still, she was determined to enter the skating competition.

Dear God, she prayed, *everything is so mixed up. Please help me.*

❋ ❋ ❋ ❋ ❋

Shannon decided not to bring up the subject at the dinner table that evening, and she was relieved that her mother didn't mention it either. She ate quietly, listening to Tiffany tell her father every detail of a school field trip that day. Although her mother glanced at her several times during the meal, Mr. Roberts was so busy being entertained by Tiffany's chatter that he didn't seem to notice that Shannon didn't enter into the conversation.

❄ ❄ ❄ ❄ ❄

Science was not the only difficult class the next day at school. It was hard to concentrate on schoolwork when she had such a major problem to solve. She hardly noticed when Mr. Terino scolded her once again for not paying attention. The human skeletal system didn't seem very important compared to her dilemma.

It seemed ages before she actually got to the rink that afternoon. Shannon laced up her skates with new determination. She was going to make the most of her practice time today. She wouldn't let anything stop her.

"Just wait 'til you see what I can do!" said Tiffany while Shannon helped her get her skates on.

"What can you do now, Tiff?" asked Shannon, trying not to sound impatient.

"I can do a toe loop jump*," Tiffany announced proudly.

"Wow! Really?" Shannon tried her best to sound impressed. "When did you learn that?"

"On Wednesday. Courtney showed me."

"I can't wait to see it," said Shannon. "But then I need to practice very hard the rest of the time."

"Okay." Tiffany looked at her sister curiously. "Shannon, why don't you like skating?"

Shannon was surprised. "What do you mean, Tiff? I love skating."

Tiffany shook her head. "You used to be fun to skate with. Now you always look mad. You don't pay attention to me."

Shannon stared at Tiffany in surprise. Suddenly, she realized that what Tiffany had said was true. She used to have so much fun at the rink. Now it was all hard work, and she didn't pay attention to anyone, not even her little sister. Maybe Tiffany felt deserted by her—as much as she felt deserted by Amy and Kristen.

Of course, she missed having her friends to practice with. But something else had happened. When she signed up for this competition, skating had become a job.

"I'm sorry, Tiff. It's just that I want to skate well in this competition. I want to prove I can be a good skater."

Tiffany looked at her with uncomprehending eyes. "I think you're good."

Shannon smiled at her sister. It was nice to know someone believed in her.

The skating session seemed to fly by. Shannon worked like she had never worked before, although she took some time out to watch her sister show her a toe loop jump.

Tiffany skated very slowly backward and planted her left toe pick into the ice behind her. She pivoted around and spread her arms to "check out" of the jump, although she never actually left the ice.

Shannon smiled, wondering whether to tell Tiffany that she hadn't really done a toe loop jump. "That was great, Tiff."

Her little sister beamed. "I'm going to be a really great skater like Jamie."

Shannon's face fell. Did everyone have to keep reminding her how wonderful Jamie was?

❋ ❋ ❋ ❋ ❋

An hour later Shannon and Tiffany were waiting for their mother to pick them up. Shannon was frustrated. She had gone through her program several times, but each time had been worse than the time before. She was beginning to feel very discouraged. Maybe she should just give up this competition. Shannon couldn't see how she could ever get ready in time.

Once again, Amy had not come to help her with her program, although she had promised to try. But Shannon hadn't really expected her.

"Stay away from the video games, Tiffany," said Shannon when her little sister headed for the machines. Kevin was there, deeply involved in a battle with aliens.

"But I'm bored," complained Tiffany, plopping down on the bench. "Mommy's late."

"Shannon, your mother just called," said Mrs. Wysong, the rink secretary, sticking her head out of the office. "Her staff meeting at school is running late. She said to tell you she'll be here as soon as she can."

Shannon turned to Tiffany. "I guess we'll have to stick around awhile."

"Oh, good," said Tiffany. "We can watch Jamie skate."

"Great!" said Shannon sarcastically. "I can't wait."

"Hi, Shannon! Hi, Tiffany!" Amy dropped her skate bag on the bench next to where the girls were sitting. Shannon hoped she hadn't heard her comment about Jamie. "I'm sorry I couldn't get here earlier. I feel awful. I keep telling you I'll come, and then I can't make it. I'm not promising anymore. I'll just show up and surprise you. I didn't think you'd still be here this late. Are you going to skate in the freestyle?"

"No, my mom is late, so we're having to wait for her," Shannon explained.

"Oh. Well, how's your competition program going?" asked Amy.

"Not too well."

"Don't worry. I always feel like that a couple of weeks before a competition. It usually comes together just in time." Amy finished lacing her skates and headed for the ice.

Shannon had her doubts whether her competition program was going to come together, but Amy's encouragement made her feel better. Tiffany had escaped to watch the video games, and Shannon was alone. There was nothing much to do except watch the freestyle skaters.

There were about a dozen skaters on the ice, including Amy, Kristen, Kevin, and Jamie. Most of them were advanced skaters—at least they seemed pretty advanced to Shannon. She saw several kids doing double jumps. However, Jamie stood out among them all.

Shannon watched while Jamie went through her competition program. From the lobby of the rink, she could just barely hear the music, a very fast Hungarian folk piece. Jamie skated with such speed and strength that most of the skaters went to the side to watch rather than try to stay out of her way.

Jamie seemed to enjoy the audience. As she performed the intricate footwork*, double jump combinations, and double axel, she grew more energetic and expressive. Shannon couldn't help but be impressed. It was easy to tell that Jamie was a very talented skater.

Shannon sat down and turned away from the ice before Jamie finished her program. She felt more discouraged than ever. How could she ever hope to compete against girls like Jamie? No wonder Jamie had told her she could never be a top skater. It would take years before Shannon could do all those moves. And by that time, Jamie would be even better.

Shannon wondered if she should just give up. Maybe it really was too late for her. She thought that by competing in this competition with her friends, she could prove to them and to everybody that she could be one of them. Now she realized that even if she competed, it would never be the same. Shannon would always be behind, no matter how hard she worked.

"Hi, Shannon." She turned to see Mrs. Lee sitting on the bench opposite her, putting on her skates.

Shannon forced a smile. "Hi, Mrs. Lee. What are you doing here?"

"This was the only time I could skate today, so I thought I would try to get in a freestyle session."

An adult skater on a freestyle? Shannon thought freestyles were just for kids.

Mrs. Lee seemed to read her thoughts. She laughed softly. "I guess I seem like an old lady to be skating in a freestyle with all the kids, don't I?"

"Oh, no," Shannon said quickly.

"You know, I started skating when I was your age."

"My age?"

"Yes. I wish I hadn't stopped," she said.

Shannon was instantly attentive. "Why did you quit?"

Mrs. Lee pulled on a pair of gloves and smiled. "I got discouraged. All the other girls my age were so much more advanced than I was. I felt funny doing jumps the little kids were doing."

Shannon could hardly believe her ears. "You felt that way, too?"

Her friend nodded. "Maybe if I hadn't stopped skating, I could have learned to skate like that girl." She pointed to Jamie, who was doing an impressive spread eagle* in a huge circle around the ice.

Shannon looked out at Jamie, then turned back to Mrs. Lee. "Why did you start skating again?" she asked.

"I just loved being on the ice." She looked out at the ice surface. "I guess I'll be skating when I'm eighty, if I can still walk."

Shannon sighed. "I would really like to be a champion skater like Jamie, but I guess it's too late for me."

Now it was Mrs. Lee's turn to look surprised. "Well, I suppose it all depends on what you think a champion is."

Shannon felt confused. "Why, you're a champion if you win a national competition or the Olympics, I guess."

"A lot of great skaters never go to the Olympics—or even win any championships." She looked hard at Shannon. "Why did you start skating, Shannon?"

"Well, because it was fun. I liked being on the ice." Shannon smiled, remembering the first time she ever skated. "I liked the idea of doing ballet on ice."

"That's the only good reason to skate, Shannon. Very few people will win gold medals, but everyone who works hard to achieve her or his goals is really a champion." She slipped on her skate guards. "If I had known that when I was your age, I never would have quit skating. May I tell you a story?"

Shannon nodded.

Mrs. Lee continued. "Some of the girls at my rink were not very nice. They yelled at me when I was in their way, and they wouldn't let me practice my program. They were traveling to skating competitions. I felt left out."

"Sometimes I feel like that," said Shannon.

"I know." Mrs. Lee smiled. "Finally, I gave up. I didn't think I could ever be as good as those other girls, so I quit trying. After I quit skating, I was very lonely. I began to study the Bible, and I learned what it means to be a true champion. The Bible tells us that there is nothing more important than serving Jesus. If we follow Him, we can be champions whether we ever win medals or not.

"That's when I decided that I would try to always be kind to everyone, even if they are not kind to me. It isn't always easy, but I ask God to help me treat everyone like Jesus would. That is much more important than how good a skater I am."

"But now you're a really good skater, too," said Shannon.

Mrs. Lee laughed. "I learned something about that, too. Something I wish I had known at your age."

Shannon listened attentively.

"I learned to trust God with my skating," said Mrs. Lee. "Now I ask Him to help me skate my best when I compete and to help me honor Him."

"I never thought about doing that," said Shannon.

Mrs. Lee headed for the ice. "Don't give up on your dreams like I did, Shannon. But remember why you're skating and ask God to help you. You'll find you won't feel so left out."

Shannon knew Mrs. Lee was right. She realized she had not done all she could to be kind to Jamie or to keep her friendship with Amy and Kristen. She had been selfish and deceitful. Shannon knew she had some serious thinking to do.

Thirteen

Shannon thought a lot about what Mrs. Lee had said. She knew in her heart that her friend was right about what makes a champion. But she also knew she had a real problem. First, she needed to tell her parents what she had done.

All through supper that evening, she thought about what she needed to do. Her mother had made lasagna, her favorite, but Shannon wasn't hungry. She stared at her plate, playing with her fork.

"Shannon, you've hardly touched your supper," said Mrs. Roberts, glancing at Shannon's plate.

"I know. I guess I'm just not hungry." Shannon picked up her fork and speared a piece of lasagna.

"I'll eat yours," volunteered Tiffany.

"That won't be necessary," said her father firmly.

Shannon put down her fork. "I have something important to tell you." She paused a moment, searching for the right words. "I skipped ballet class on Tuesday so that I could get more skating practice. I'm really sorry I lied to you and everybody else." Shannon stopped, fighting back tears. Even though she was afraid of what her parents might do, she felt better having confessed.

Her parents looked at each other without speaking. Finally, Mrs. Roberts spoke. "We know about it, Shannon. We're glad you decided to tell us the truth."

Shannon looked surprised. "How did you find out?"

"Madame Junot called me Tuesday afternoon when you didn't show up for class," said her mother, "and I asked Tiffany what she knew."

Shannon shot her sister a look.

"Don't blame Tiffany," said Mrs. Roberts. "She had no choice but to tell me the truth—and you had no right to ask her to lie for you."

"I'm sorry, everyone," said Shannon. "It was awful. I felt so guilty. I couldn't do anything right. I wish I hadn't done it. I'll take whatever punishment you decide."

"You know what you did was wrong, and we don't want it to happen again. Originally, we were not going to allow you any telephone or television privileges for three weeks. Since you came forward and told us the truth, we will reduce that to two weeks," said her mother. Her mother continued. "However, I think you're going to be too busy to miss those privileges." She looked at Mr. Roberts, who smiled.

He turned to Shannon. "We think we have a solution to the problem of your ballet recital practices."

Shannon looked up hopefully. "Really?"

Her mother spoke. "We realize that skating and ballet are both important to you. I checked with the rink. There are freestyle times available in the morning before school. You can skate then, at least until after the competition. And Coach Barnes said she could give you your lessons in the morning."

"Lessons?" asked Shannon.

"Yes," said Mr. Roberts. "Your mother and I have decided to allow you to take an extra thirty-minute lesson a week until the competition."

Shannon jumped up from the table and threw her arms around her mother and then her father. "You really mean it? I can skate the freestyles with Amy and Kristen?"

"But only for this competition. After that, we'll see. Skating and ballet are both expensive. I think you're going to have to make some decisions about what is most important."

"What about me?" asked Tiffany. "Can I skate with Shannon?"

Her mother shook her head. "No, you can keep skating in the afternoon. You wouldn't want to leave April and Courtney, would you?"

Tiffany frowned. "April and Courtney are just beginners. I want to skate with the good skaters."

Shannon giggled. Even Tiffany already had an attitude.

Mr. Roberts gave Shannon a stern look, then turned to Tiffany. "Coach Barnes said she would rather have you skate with the other girls your age."

"Oh, well," said Tiffany. "If Coach Barnes said so, I guess it's okay."

"When can I start?" asked Shannon eagerly.

"Monday morning," said her mother. "And now, let's not hear any more talk about skipping the ballet recital."

Shannon's lasagna was getting cold, but she hardly noticed. She picked up her fork and dug in, too excited to realize what she was eating.

Her parents had solved both her problems. She would be able to skate in the competition and still dance the solo in the recital. And as a bonus she would be able to skate with Amy and Kristen again, since both of them skated in the morning before school.

❊ ❊ ❊ ❊ ❊

Skating in the morning freestyles was hard at first. In the public session, most of the skaters were beginners. There weren't usually a lot of figure skaters. However, in the morning freestyle sessions most of the skaters were more advanced. Everyone was flying here and there at high speeds. At first Shannon found it difficult to practice—she spent most of Monday morning dodging other skaters and fielding dirty looks. Rather than feeling like one of the figure skaters, she felt more like a beginner than ever. Exasperated, she retreated to the side of the rink.

Kristen noticed her confusion and skated over to her. "Skating in freestyles is hard at first," she said with an encouraging smile.

"I feel like I'm in everybody's way," moaned Shannon.

Kristen grinned. "I know. I used to feel the same way. It'll get better."

Gradually, Shannon learned how to maneuver around the other skaters. She learned to pay attention when she heard someone's program music; other skaters are expected to stay out of the way of a skater practicing a program. Skating through her own program was scary. Shannon felt as though all the skaters and coaches on the ice were watching.

For the next few days, Shannon practiced harder than she thought possible. In order to skate before school, she had to get up much earlier. In the afternoons she had ballet rehearsals. By the time she got home and ate supper, she was almost too tired to do her homework. That wasn't a problem in most of her classes, but Shannon was falling behind in science.

One day Mr. Terino handed back a test he had recently given to the class, and Shannon was shocked to find she had failed. Although she didn't always make straight A's, she had always been a fairly good student. Never in her life had she failed a test.

She sat at her desk staring at the test paper in disbelief. "Shannon, you are capable of doing much better," said Mr. Terino. "Perhaps you need to put aside some of your other activities in favor of spending more time on your homework." He continued handing out tests to the other students.

What was she going to do? Shannon already spent more time on science than on any of her other homework assignments. If her grades didn't improve, she might fail the class. With the competition and the ballet recital both coming up, she barely had time to get everything done. There was no way she could spend extra time on science homework.

Shannon put her test away and pulled out her notebook to begin taking notes on Mr. Terino's lecture. Right now there was nothing much she could do. Science would just have to wait until after the competition and the recital. Maybe then she could work hard enough to bring her grades up.

✳ ✳ ✳ ✳ ✳

Jamie looked up from lacing her skates and smiled when Shannon came into the lobby of the rink the next morning. "Hi, Shannon," she said.

Shannon was a little surprised at Jamie's friendliness. She had been coming in the morning for a week, but this was the first time Jamie had spoken to her. "Hi, Jamie," she answered, with just a hint of suspicion in her voice.

"How do you like skating in the morning?" Jamie asked.

Shannon sat down and pulled her skates out of her bag. "I like it, except that I'm really tired in the evenings." She tugged at a lace. "Too tired to study," she added.

Jamie nodded. "Sometimes it is hard to get all my homework done, too."

"I've got this tyrant of a teacher for science," said Shannon. "He doesn't believe a person should do anything in life except homework for his class."

Jamie was sympathetic. "That's too bad. And science is such a cool subject, too."

"I know. It used to be my favorite subject. But not anymore."

"What are you studying right now?" asked Jamie.

"The human skeletal system."

"Really? I've got some great books on the human body. I don't know if they'd be any help, but you can borrow them if you'd like."

Maybe Jamie's not really such a snob, Shannon thought. "Thanks. I need all the help I can get."

"I'll bring them tomorrow," Jamie promised. She gave a final tug to her skate laces and stood up. "It's time to hit the ice." She made a face. "And I probably will, too."

Shannon smiled. Maybe Jamie wasn't so bad after all.

"See you on the ice!" Jamie called out as she went through the lobby doors.

Shannon was having a lesson with Coach Barnes that morning, and she wasn't looking forward to it. She knew her coach wouldn't be happy with her skating. Shannon had worked as hard as she possibly could, but with only a few days left before the competition, her program was not coming together. She just wasn't comfortable with all the new moves yet.

"Okay, Shannon, let's see how you're doing," said her coach at the beginning of Shannon's lesson. After working individually on some of the jumps and spins, the coach put on her program tape.

Shannon skated to her starting position, her heart beating fast. Although this wasn't an actual competition, she felt almost as nervous. She wanted more than anything to skate impressively enough to convince the other skaters that she could be one of them.

The music started, and Shannon focused on performing every move as well as she could. However, as she continued through the program, she grew farther and farther behind the music until she felt as though she was rushing to catch up. When she came to her final move, she threw herself into the sit spin and ended up on her bottom. Red-faced, she scrambled to her feet and struck her ending pose, a full five seconds after the end of the music.

Shannon dreaded facing her coach after that dismal run-through. She knew she had not skated well, and the competition was less than a week away.

To her surprise, her coach's comments were encouraging. "Well, that wasn't bad—but next time let's end on your feet!" She grinned at Shannon. "Watch that entrance into the spin, and you'll be fine."

Shannon was unconvinced. "I've practiced and practiced, and I just can't seem to get this program right," she complained. Her eyes were troubled. "I don't know if I should even do this competition."

Coach Barnes grew serious. "I warned you it was going to be tough. On the other hand, I can tell you've worked hard. You're really doing very well."

Shannon hesitated, but finally dared to ask, "Do you think I have any chance at all of winning a medal?"

The coach looked at her thoughtfully. "Competing is about more than just winning medals. If winning a medal is the most important thing to you, then skip this competition."

Shannon's face fell. Deep down she had known the truth, but it was tough to have her coach say it.

Coach Barnes continued. "You've worked hard and prepared, and you've learned a lot. This competition may not be exactly what you had in mind, but it will be good experience. I think you should go ahead and compete."

For a few moments, Shannon hesitated. Should she enter a competition that even her coach thought she had no chance of winning? What if she skated badly? That would be so embarrassing.

But her coach thought she should do the competition. She still had a few days left to practice, after all. Even if she skated badly, Shannon knew she would learn a lot.

She took a deep breath and nodded. "I guess I need to keep working." Shannon had a new goal for this competition—and it had nothing to do with winning a medal.

Fourteen

"Time to get up!" Tiffany jumped on Shannon's bed and began bouncing up and down.

"Stop it, Tiffany!" grumbled Shannon, sliding farther under the covers.

"You gotta get up and get ready for your competition!" Tiffany pulled at the covers.

"Oh, yeah," mumbled Shannon, now fully awake.

All week long Shannon had practiced hard for the competition, harder than she had ever practiced for anything in her life. By the time of her last practice, she almost felt ready.

She sat up in bed and closed her eyes. Mentally, she reviewed her entire program from start to finish. Was it good enough to compete? She didn't know, but her hard work had improved her skating immensely.

Shannon had never really worked hard at anything before. Things had always come pretty easily to her.

Even skating had come easily at first. For the first time in her life she had found something that was a real challenge. Whatever happened today, she felt good that she had met that challenge. Even her coach was pleased with her improvement.

The beautiful pink competition dress Amy had loaned her hung on the closet door. The last time she wore it was in her first competition. She smiled, remembering how nervous she felt before she competed. She hoped she wouldn't have such an attack of nerves today. Already she felt a little shaky.

Shannon closed her eyes and prayed, *Dear God, help me to skate my best today.* She paused a moment, then added: *And help me to skate for the right reason.*

❄ ❄ ❄ ❄ ❄

The rink where the competition was being held was huge, with two ice surfaces instead of just one. Shannon could feel the butterflies fluttering in her stomach.

"Wow! I wish I was skating!" said Tiffany, wide-eyed with wonder at the palace-like facility.

"I wish Dad could have come to see me," Shannon said.

"He hated to miss it," said her mother, "but he couldn't get anyone to take his place at the hospital."

Now that she was here, Shannon felt very nervous. While Mrs. Roberts turned in her music tape at the registration table, Shannon watched the other skaters mingling around the gigantic lobby of the skating complex.

"You're all registered and ready to go," said Mrs.

Roberts. "Why don't you two go watch the skating, while I browse through all those tables over there."

❄ ❄ ❄ ❄ ❄

As Shannon and Tiffany entered the arena, they saw Amy waving and yelling.

"Shannon, Tiffany, over here!" she called. The girls made their way to where Amy and Kristen were sitting. Shannon found a place on the bleachers for her skate bag, dress, and backpack.

"You're just in time," said Amy. "Jamie's skating next."

Tiffany smiled broadly. "Good. Jamie's the best! I'm going to be just like her."

"Poor Jamie," teased Shannon.

Tiffany made a face at her sister.

Shannon turned to her friends. "Have we missed seeing any of you guys skate?"

"Just me." Kevin dropped onto the seat beside the girls. "Too bad. You missed a great show!"

Kristen nodded. "Yes, there was this guy from Oklahoma who was wonderful!" she said, baiting Kevin. "You should have seen him . . . and cute . . ."

"Oh, him!" Kevin scowled at his sister. "He couldn't even land his double flip*!"

Kristen just grinned.

"Well, who won?" asked Shannon.

"The guy from Oklahoma!" said Amy, grinning.

"Hey! I know when I'm not wanted," said Kevin. "I think I'll go visit the snack bar."

101

Kevin had just left when the girls heard Jamie's name being announced. Jamie skated to the center of the rink and immediately took her starting position, looking cool and confident.

Shannon watched while Jamie skated through her program of double jump combinations, intricate footwork, and spins. In her costume on the ice she looked more impressive than ever. One by one she hit every jump, until she ended with the final spin combination.

Jamie made everything look so easy. Shannon was sure even Amy and Kristen must be a little envious.

Tiffany was thoroughly impressed. "I'm going to skate just like that!"

Kristen agreed. "She'll win first, I'm sure."

"She even landed her triple toe loop," said Amy. "Nobody else in the group even tried a triple jump."

Maybe one day I'll be doing triple toe loops, thought Shannon. She turned to her friends. "When do you guys skate?"

"Not until later this afternoon," said Kristen. "But we wanted to be here to watch you and Jamie."

"And Kevin," added Amy.

"I didn't care about seeing Kevin skate," said Kristen with a smile. "I see him all the time."

Mrs. Roberts came in and sat near the girls. She looked at her watch. "It's only an hour before you're scheduled to skate. Maybe you'd better get changed."

Shannon suddenly felt sick. Was she ready for this? She picked up the garment bag with her costume and the backpack with her makeup and hair supplies. "Anybody want to come with me?"

Amy carried Shannon's skate bag, and Kristen went along, too. They found a dressing room where she changed into her tights and the pink skating dress. Shannon carefully put on some eye makeup, blush, and lipstick so that her face would show up across the big ice surface.

Kristen helped Shannon fix her hair into a small knot and carefully secured it with bobby pins. Then she put on a pink scrunchie that matched the dress.

"You don't seem as nervous as you did for the last competition," commented Amy.

"Actually, I feel worse," admitted Shannon. "My stomach is really queasy. I'm scared I might blow the whole program."

"You won't blow it," Kristen assured her. "We all feel like that sometimes, but you've worked really hard. You'll do fine."

"Thanks," said Shannon, "but I'll be glad when it's over."

"We'll both be praying for you," said Kristen.

The waiting was the hard part. Shannon thought her turn to skate would never come. Amy and Kristen tried to keep her company by making conversation and cracking jokes, but Shannon only half heard them. Her mind was focused on only one thing: her ninety seconds on the ice.

After the warmup, Shannon waited by the entrance with her coach. Her legs were like jelly, and for a moment she was afraid she wouldn't remember her program. Worst of all, she felt as though she might throw up any minute. She would have given anything to be somewhere else.

Suddenly, she saw Mrs. Lee in the crowd looking on. As she looked, Mrs. Lee caught her eye and gave her an encouraging smile. Surprised, Shannon smiled back. She hadn't realized her friend would be there, but for some reason she felt less nervous now. She remembered what Mrs. Lee had told her that day at the rink about asking God to help her with her skating.

Dear God, please help me to remember why I'm skating. Help me to skate my best. Help me to skate for You instead of for medals. And help me not to embarrass myself. Amen.

"Please welcome Shannon Roberts," said the announcer. Shannon gave a quick glance at her coach for reassurance and skated into her starting position. Although she still felt shaky, she put on a brave smile and waited for her music.

The familiar music filled the arena, and Shannon began skating. She hardly had to think about her routine—all her hard work had paid off. Steadily, she skated through her program, landing every jump from the waltz jump–toe loop jump combination to the salchow. By the time she landed the flip jump, Shannon was really enjoying her program. The landing was a little shaky, but it was pretty good for a jump she had just learned. The smile on her face was real. *Hey, this is fun,* she thought.

Her hardest move was the sit spin, which she managed to complete with just enough rotations, and she struck her final ending pose with a triumphant smile. She couldn't believe she had gotten through her program so well!

Her coach was pleased with her performance. "Great job!" she said when Shannon stepped off the ice.

Her mother and little sister were waiting with hugs and congratulations; Amy, Kristen, and Jamie were there, too.

"You skated great!" said Amy excitedly.

"I can't believe I did it!" exclaimed Shannon, smiling with relief. "I'm so glad it's over."

The girls laughed. "I know just how you feel!" said Jamie.

"*We* don't!" said Kristen. "We have to wait until this afternoon to compete."

Shannon felt a tap on her shoulder; she turned to see Kevin give her a "thumbs-up" sign. From Kevin, that was a real compliment!

"I knew you could do it." Shannon recognized Mrs. Lee's soft accent. She turned to receive a hug from her friend.

"I didn't know you would be here," said Shannon. "Are you competing today?"

Mrs. Lee shook her head. "Not this time. I came to see *you!*"

Shannon felt a warm glow. She couldn't believe her friend came just to watch her skate. "Thank you for coming," she said, smiling broadly.

It was hard to wait for the results. Shannon tried not to hope for too much. There were nine other girls in her group, and she knew that some of them had skated very well and three of them had even landed an axel in their program.

Still, in spite of her good intentions, it was disappointing to find her name listed in sixth place. Coach Barnes noticed Shannon's disappointment and said, "You skated a great program, but most of these girls have been skating longer than you."

"I know," said Shannon. "I guess I really wasn't ready, was I?"

Coach Barnes patted her on the back. "This was a great experience for you, Shannon, and it pushed you to really improve your skating. I think we can call it a success."

Shannon smiled, pleased with the unexpected praise. "I didn't think it could ever be fun skating for judges, but it was. I guess I'm glad I did it."

Her friends were not quite as understanding of the rankings. "Those judges must have been blind!" complained Amy. Kristen agreed. "I know you skated better than sixth place."

Only Jamie was more realistic. "I think sixth place is super for somebody who's only been skating a few months. Just think how well you'll do next time."

It was nice that Amy and Kristen were so supportive, but Shannon knew that Jamie was right. She would be more competitive in a few months.

Shannon decided it didn't matter how the judges ranked her. She knew she had skated better than she ever had before. She would have plenty of opportunities to win medals in the future. But for right now, she just enjoyed skating, and she was grateful for the chance to skate.

In the meantime, it was fun watching the other skaters compete, and hearing their music choices gave Shannon lots of ideas for programs and costumes. She decided she was really looking forward to competing again.

Finally, it was Amy's and Kristen's turns to skate. Just as at the last competition, the two girls were having to compete against each other. Shannon wanted both to win first place, but she knew that was impossible. "I hope you both skate your very best," she told them.

She and Jamie went back to find a seat with her mother and Tiffany. They waited anxiously for their friends to skate.

Kristen was the first to skate, and she performed her program beautifully as always. Nobody worked as hard on her skating as Kristen did, and when she competed, she did every move with perfection. She landed several double jumps, including two jump combinations; in-between her jumps there was great footwork, beautiful spirals and spread eagles*, and combination spins*. Her only mistake was putting her other foot down when landing the double lutz jump*. A clean landing must be on one foot.

Shannon and Jamie clapped loudly when she fin-ished. *How could anybody top that? Poor Amy,* thought Shannon. *It would be hard to beat that performance.*

However, when Amy's turn came, she burst onto the ice. Her determination showed on her face. The music was jazzy and energetic, and that's how Amy skated. She landed one jump after another, skating her heart out with a big smile on her face.

Amy finished with a few dance steps at the end of her program, and Shannon and Jamie cheered so loudly that Amy heard them. She turned and smiled happily in their direction.

When the results were posted, Amy was second and Kristen was third. They were all thrilled. Jamie had won a first place medal, so it had been a successful day. "Shannon, we want you to come celebrate with us this evening," said Kristen.

Shannon looked at her mother, who nodded. "They've already checked with me. I'll drop you off at Kristen's house at seven tonight."

"Can I go?" asked Tiffany, looking at her mother.

Mrs. Roberts shook her head, but Kristen said, "We'd love to have Tiffany, if it's okay."

Tiffany beamed, but her mother looked doubtful.

"Tiffany's one of us," put in Amy. "We can't have a celebration without her."

Jamie put her arm around the little girl and nodded. "Please, Mrs. Roberts, let her come."

Tiffany nodded vigorously, grinning at her mother. Mrs. Roberts laughed. "All right. Since everybody wants you, you can go." She turned to the other girls. "But just remember, you asked for it!"

Amy whispered something in Tiffany's ear and she giggled. "Don't tell," warned Amy, putting her finger to her mouth.

"All right," whispered Tiffany, looking at Shannon.

By now Shannon was getting suspicious. "What do you guys have up your sleeves?"

Jamie whistled, while Amy replied, "Oh, nothing much."

Kristen gave the others a warning glare. "We'll see you guys at seven, okay?"

Shannon wondered what was going on. Her friends were definitely acting a little strange. It might have something to do with Jamie's surprise party, but Jamie seemed to be in on the secret.

"Better be on time," said Jamie. "You wouldn't want to miss anything." She grinned mischievously.

It was time to leave. Shannon smiled a little uncomfortably at her friends as she followed her mother and sister out of the rink.

What was going on?

Fifteen

Tiffany giggled all the way home. "Settle down!" said her mother. "I need to concentrate on my driving."

"I think she had too much of that mixed soda thing they were making," said Shannon, giving her sister a meaningful look.

"I did not!" protested Tiffany.

"It's nearly six thirty now," said Mrs. Roberts. "You girls need to hurry to get ready in time."

"I wonder what they're planning?" Shannon asked aloud. "Tiffany, you know something, don't you?"

Tiffany just giggled and covered her mouth with her hands. "I can't tell you!" was her muffled comment.

"You do know something! Mom, make her tell!"

Mrs. Roberts shook her head. "I'm afraid you'll just have to wait and see."

Now Shannon was really suspicious. Her mother knew something, too. That was obvious, but Shannon knew better than to try to get anything out of her. She would just have to wait.

❄ ✳ ❄ ✳ ❄

"Surprise!" shouted Amy, Kristen, and Jamie as soon as Shannon walked in the door. "Happy birthday!"

Shannon caught her breath. The surprise party was for her, not Jamie! She stood in the doorway a few moments, taking everything in. There were balloons, streamers, and a huge banner with *"Happy Birthday."*

Tiffany scooted past her and into Kristen's house. "Where's the cake?" she said, looking all around.

"Tiffany, you're being rude!" scolded Shannon. She turned to her friends. "How did you know it was my birthday?"

Amy grinned. "We have ways!" she said significantly.

"I told them!" volunteered Tiffany, coming back from the kitchen. "Come see the cake!"

"Food! Is that all you think about?" asked Shannon, as she sank into the nearest large chair.

Tiffany shrugged. "I'm always hungry."

The girls laughed. "Okay, Tiff," said Kristen. "We'll eat in a few minutes. My mom ordered us some pizza."

"Were you really surprised?" asked Amy. She sat on the floor and reached for a handful of the snack mix on the coffee table. "We were so afraid you'd find out about the party."

Shannon hesitated. "Uh . . . well, I knew you guys were up to something . . ."

111

Amy's face fell. "Oh, no! Did Tiffany give us away?"

Tiffany was munching on some popcorn, but she stopped to protest. "I didn't tell!"

Shannon defended her sister. "No, Tiffany didn't tell me anything. I overheard you guys at the rink one day talking about a surprise party. But I thought the party was for Jamie."

"For me?" asked Jamie in surprise. "Why would they give me a party? My birthday's not until June."

"I didn't know that," explained Shannon. "It's just that I hardly ever see you guys anymore. I thought—"

"You thought we weren't your friends anymore?" asked Amy, pretending to pout. "Just because we didn't see you every day?"

Shannon felt confused. She tried to explain. "Well, you guys are all such good skaters, and I'm just a beginner. I thought you didn't want to hang around with me anymore."

"Just because we've been skating longer than you?" Amy looked offended. "Oh, *puh-leeze!*"

"We'd be your friends even if you didn't skate," said Kristen. "It's just nicer that you love to skate, too."

"Yeah, you should have heard them," said Jamie. "All they've talked about since I came here was how fast you'd learned all your jumps. They talked about you so much it kind of made *me* a little jealous."

Suddenly, Shannon laughed. "I can't believe it. You were jealous of me?" Then she grew more serious. "I've been a little jealous myself—of *all* of you."

"Jealous of us?" asked Kristen. She looked confused. "Why were you jealous of us?"

Shannon was a little embarrassed at having said so much. "You all have been skating for so long, and I'm just a beginner. I guess I felt sort of left out."

It was Jamie's turn to be embarrassed. "I'm sorry about what I said—that you could never be a great skater. Some champion skaters did start late."

"That's okay," said Shannon.

All the girls were quiet for a moment. Finally, Kristen spoke. "I guess we all need to say we're sorry. We didn't mean to leave you out of things. We were just busy getting ready for the competition."

"I'm sorry, too," added Amy. "I promised to help you with your program, but I never showed up at the rink to do it. I guess I thought you didn't really want my help. You didn't seem to want to talk to us anymore."

"Sometimes I didn't," admitted Shannon. "I was trying so hard to show you I could be a good skater, I forgot to be a friend."

The girls looked at one another. No one spoke. Even Tiffany was quiet.

Finally, Jamie spoke. "That's how it starts." The girls looked at her curiously as she continued. "I've been to lots of competitions, and everybody's your friend at first. Then it happens. You start landing a new jump, or you win a medal, and suddenly you don't have any friends."

"That's what happened to Mrs. Lee," said Shannon softly. "She started skating when she was my age, but some other girls were really mean to her. She was so hurt that she quit skating."

"Wow! I never knew that," said Kristen.

"What made her start skating again?" asked Jamie.

"It was years before she would get on the ice again," said Shannon. "Then one day, after she was grown up, she went skating, and she remembered how much she loved just being on the ice. She decided that was more important than competing and winning medals."

"It's terrible that those girls made her quit. She might have been a world champion," Amy said.

Shannon was thoughtful. "I told her that, and she laughed. She said she never thought about that. She is only sorry she missed all those years of being on the ice."

"That sounds like something she'd say," said Kristen. "I want to be just like her. I love to watch her skate, and she's always kind to everybody."

"She told me about that, too," said Shannon. "She said when she stopped skating, she was really lonely. She started studying her Bible, and she learned that Jesus wanted us to treat other people just as He would treat them. She decided to treat everybody like Jesus would."

"And she does, too," said Kristen. "I've known her a long time, and I've never seen her be unkind to anyone."

"That's what I want to be like," said Shannon. "I want to be a good skater, but not if it means losing my friends."

"I have an idea," said Jamie. "A lot of people think figure skaters are just out to get each other. Let's promise each other to stay friends no matter what and to treat everybody the way Jesus would."

"I promise!" said Shannon.

"I promise," agreed Amy and Kristen.

"What about me?" asked Tiffany. "I'm a skater, too." She jumped up from her place at the coffee table, spilling popcorn all over the floor. "I want to treat people nice, and I want to be world champion."

Kristen laughed. "Yes, Tiffany, you can promise, too."

Tiffany sat down solemnly with the group. She attempted to make a serious face, which looked so comical that the girls had a hard time not bursting into laughter. "I promise."

"Anyone for pizza?" asked Mrs. Grant, coming into the living room. "Oh, am I interrupting something important?"

"It's okay, Mom," said Kristen. "Let's eat, guys!"

The girls quickly ate the pizza. It was sausage and mushroom—Shannon's favorite. *How did they know?* she wondered. While she ate, she realized that she was happier than she had been for weeks. She had her friends back; in fact, they had been her friends all along.

Sixteen

The ballet recital was only three weeks after Shannon's birthday party. It was a busy three weeks. Ballet rehearsals went late, and she worked hard getting ready for her solo.

Shannon continued to skate, but only two mornings a week before school. She spent her afternoons in rehearsals for the ballet. When she came home from ballet practice, there was barely time to eat supper and get her homework done before she had to go to bed at nine.

It was still a tough schedule. Shannon frequently found herself yawning in class, especially science. In spite of that, she was doing better in Mr. Terino's class. Jamie had not only loaned her books to help, but had helped her with her homework. Shannon had caught up and had actually made a ninety on the last test. Mr. Terino had scribbled "Well done" on the top of the test paper.

"I told you if you just studied harder, you'd do better in this class," was Mr. Terino's comment when he handed her the test paper. Shannon just smiled. There was no need to tell Terino the Terrible that her better grades resulted from the help she had received from Jamie.

Shannon discovered that Jamie wasn't a snob at all. In fact, she spent time on weekends helping Shannon with her skating. During one of her private lessons, her coach commented on how much her loop and flip jumps had improved. "The difference is just amazing," said her coach, shaking her head in disbelief. Shannon just grinned. Jamie was a great coach! And a great friend.

Extra rehearsals before the recital left Shannon exhausted. Although she was getting excited about her solo, she knew she couldn't keep up this schedule much longer. She was relieved when the big day finally arrived.

Amy, Kristen, and Jamie were all coming to see her dance. Even Kevin suggested he might consider showing up.

"You're going to a ballet?" asked Kristen. "You've never been interested before. Aren't you afraid the other guys will tease you?"

"*Russian* skaters always go to the ballet," he said defensively.

Kristen gave him a funny look. "Do you mind if he comes?" she asked Shannon and then laughed. "He thinks he's a Russian."

"No, of course not." Shannon was a little embarrassed. She wondered why Kevin wanted to come to see her. He had never seemed to pay any attention to her ballet before.

Getting ready for the recital, Shannon found herself almost as nervous as she had been for the skating competition. "What if I mess up?" she asked her mother anxiously while she fixed her hair. Putting up Shannon's medium-length hair for recitals was always a challenge. It took a ton of styling gel and hairspray to plaster her hair into the severe traditional pulled-back style Madame Junot required for performances.

Shannon finished putting on her stage makeup and took down the garment bag with the costume for her solo. It was beautiful, with a white bodice trimmed with beading and lace and a full three-quarter-length skirt. It was not very comfortable, but Shannon felt like a princess when she had it on.

Her mother picked up the ballet bag and the costume. "You'll be wonderful, of course," she assured her. "I wish I could have had the opportunities you've had. I would have loved to have taken ballet classes when I was growing up."

Shannon looked at her mother in surprise. It had never occurred to her that her mother might have had dreams when she was young. "I thought you took ballet classes," she said. "I saw a picture of you in a ballet costume."

Mrs. Roberts nodded. "I know. My parents let me take ballet for a year when I was about eight or nine. Then they couldn't afford it anymore, so I had to quit." She sighed. "I was brokenhearted, and they promised they'd try to let me start back later, but somehow it never happened."

Shannon suddenly understood why her mother cared so much about her ballet classes. She was afraid Shannon would always regret it if she quit. "Mom, I really like ballet. I don't want to quit, but I love skating, too. If I had to quit skating, I would feel just like you did about having to quit ballet."

Mrs. Roberts looked at her thoughtfully. "I know. The competition made me realize how important skating is to you. You have worked so hard, getting up early in the morning and giving up all your free time to fit everything in."

"I just wish I didn't have to choose," said Shannon.

Her mother smiled and gave Shannon a hug. "Maybe you won't. If you learn to balance things and do them for the right reason, maybe you can do both. Anyway, I'm really proud of you. You'll dance beautifully tonight, I know."

Shannon was so happy she forgot about being nervous. Her mother finally understood about skating! God had answered her prayers. *Thank You, Lord,* she prayed silently. *Now help me to skate and dance for You.*

✳ ✳ ✳ ✳ ✳

Waiting in the wings for her final cue, Shannon thought about all her friends and family in the audience. Mom, Dad, and Tiffany were always there for her. And Amy, Kristen, and Jamie—even Kevin—were there to cheer her on. She had been nervous about her performance, but having so many people who cared gave her confidence.

When she finished, Shannon knew she had performed better than she had ever performed before. There was a burst of applause, and she smiled broadly. Even Madame Junot would be pleased with her.

"You were great!" said Darcy after the performance. Shannon smiled. "Thanks."

Everyone was waiting for her by the stage door after the recital was over. Even Kevin was there, with a bouquet of pink carnations. Shannon blushed as she accepted the flowers.

"Someday, I want to be a ballerina-skater, just like you," Tiffany said.

Shannon gave Tiffany a hug. Sometimes little sisters said just the right thing. She had never felt so happy. She realized she had friends who cared and a family that loved her. She didn't feel left out in the cold anymore.